MW00461017

Praise for Bianca D'Arc's
Wolf Quest

"This one is a hot and passionate romance, with lots of danger and action that kept me on the edge of my seat."
~ *Long and Short Reviews*

"*Wolf Quest* is another fantastic book in this series. I loved every minute of this sexy, action packed tale."
~ *Night Owl Reviews*

"Author Bianca D'Arc never disappoints her readers by throwing out less than quality work. *Wolf Quest* is definitely one worth reading and keeping."
~ *Fresh Fiction*

Look for these titles by
Bianca D'Arc

Now Available:

Wolf Quest

Bianca D'Arc

To Kella,
Welcome to the
D'Arc side!

Bianca
D'Arc

SAMHAIN
PUBLISHING

Samhain Publishing, Ltd.
11821 Mason Montgomery Road, 4B
Cincinnati, OH 45249
www.samhainpublishing.com

Wolf Quest
Copyright © 2013 by Bianca D'Arc
Print ISBN: 978-1-61922-280-9
Digital ISBN: 978-1-61922-087-4

Editing by Heidi Moore
Cover by Angela Waters

This book is a work of fiction. The names, characters, places, and incidents are products of the writer's imagination or have been used fictitiously and are not to be construed as real. Any resemblance to persons, living or dead, actual events, locale or organizations is entirely coincidental.

All Rights Are Reserved. No part of this book may be used or reproduced in any manner whatsoever without written permission, except in the case of brief quotations embodied in critical articles and reviews.

First Samhain Publishing, Ltd. electronic publication: December 2013
First Samhain Publishing, Ltd. print publication: December 2014

Dedication

This book is for my family, as always. I would never have been able to do any of this without their love and support.

Chapter One

"You hear that, Jess?" Arlo said over the tactical radios his small team employed.

The sound of breaking glass and the crash of furniture came from inside the farmhouse.

"I hear it. I think the subtle approach just went out the window. Let's go." Jesse moved on the backdoor even as he gave the order. He knew his team was doing the same on other approaches. They would storm the house and neutralize whatever threat was inside, probably frightening the girl they'd been sent to check on, but that couldn't be avoided now.

Something was going on in there. Some kind of struggle. That much noise indicated nothing less than a full-throttle fight in progress.

Jesse kicked the door in and found what he'd expected, though not exactly the scenario he'd anticipated. There was a struggle going on all right, but the two men attacking the young lovely in her nightgown were definitely on the defensive. One was already out cold, slumped against the far wall, while the other was face down on the kitchen floor, his arm twisted behind him in what had to be an excruciating position. The woman crouching over his back had a fierce expression on her lovely face and her dark hair flipped out to the side almost in slow motion as she turned her head to look at Jesse.

"What do you want?" She couldn't have growled any better if she'd been a female werewolf in half-shifted battle form.

The thought made Jesse grin as he aimed his weapon at the ground, away from her.

"We thought you might need some help, but I see you have

matters in hand here."

"We?" she asked, arching one eyebrow as she pulled the man's arm a little tighter. The guy grunted in pain but she wasn't letting up.

Jesse gave the signal over his tactical radio and the rest of the team appeared in the hall leading to the kitchen. The woman would be able to see them if she looked up, but the dude on the ground with his cheek pressed into the linoleum wouldn't. Jesse gestured toward the hall with his eyes, hoping she'd get the message.

Wonder of wonders, she did. This girl was on the ball. Of course, he shouldn't have expected anything less from Sally's cousin. His brother's new wife had already proven to be more than a match for a male Alpha werewolf.

And Jesse was definitely Alpha. And male. And a werewolf.

All his senses were standing on end in the gorgeous female's presence. A bare hint of her scent wafted to him and his hormones raged.

Whoa. Down boy.

"Ma'am..." Jesse made himself get back to business. "We've been pursuing these boys. They're wanted in connection with a kidnapping in Wyoming. I'm sorry we had to barge into your home, but I thought you might need assistance. As team leader, I take full responsibility, and I promise we'll repair any damage our entry may have caused." He glanced significantly back at the kitchen door. It was badly splintered and still swinging slightly on its hinges.

She didn't ease off the man on the floor. "Look, buddy, I don't know you. For all I know you could be working for these guys, just waiting for me to let this one go."

"While I applaud your caution, in this instance it's misplaced. If you'll allow me?" He didn't wait for an answer before pulling a dart gun from the holster on his thigh and plugging the struggling man with sleep juice.

She didn't even have time to blink, which was a good thing. Jesse sure as hell didn't want to tranq her by mistake. Oh, no. He wanted her awake and spitting at him. He wanted the chance to try to gentle her. To woo her.

Woo her? Where the hell had that come from? Damn. She was every bit as attractive as her cousin and twice as alluring to Jesse's senses. He'd thought his brother was a lucky man when he'd found Sally, but the mild envy he'd felt had nothing on the downright possessive streak that stirred in him at seeing Maria Garibaldi in her nightdress.

The dude under her went slack as the fast-acting drug kicked in.

"What did you just do?" she accused, outrage in her silky voice. Damn. He could listen to her for hours and never tire.

This thought from a man who found most women intensely annoying when they started to chatter? He was in trouble. Big trouble.

"He'll wake in a few hours. I figured you wouldn't mind since you knocked the other one out cold." He glanced at the other man, still slumped against the wall. Signaling his men to enter the kitchen, he stepped closer to Maria. "We'll take these guys off your hands, ma'am."

Maria stood faster than he would have credited as he stepped forward. She was really quick for a human. Maybe her alleged magical ancestry gave her some physical advantages.

"You can have them, but I'm not going anywhere. And you can think again if you expect me to agree to anything else you may have in mind."

He holstered the dart gun and held his hands out, palms up in the intergalactic gesture of *I come in peace.*

"We mean you no harm, Maria." Her chin jerked up defiantly when he used her first name. "It's okay. We really have been following these guys for a couple of weeks. Two of their friends kidnapped a young boy in Wyoming. We got those two, but these guys have been leading us cross-country."

Arlo and Len had secured the unconscious man's wrists and feet with zip ties. They'd also disarmed him while Jesse had been talking. Maria had been splitting her attention between them and Jesse for the past minute or more. She was like a caged animal, ready to strike and unsure what was coming next. He had to calm her down but he wasn't sure how.

"Why here?" she whispered. "Why me?"

Now there was a question. Jesse paused. He wasn't sure how much she knew about the magical world around her. She might be like her cousin Sally, who had been completely unaware of the *weres*, bloodletters and other kinds of magical beings living alongside the human population. Or she might know a lot more than Sally had. He'd noticed a couple of low-level wardings in Maria's backyard. Nothing that could stop a werewolf of course, but enough to let a magic user know that someone was trespassing on their land.

"Do you know what I am?" Jesse tested the waters.

To his amazement, she sniffed in his direction. That wasn't something a human would do. She looked at the man on the floor before speaking as if to make certain he was fully asleep.

"*Were?*" She didn't seem too sure of her answer.

Jesse grinned at her, letting her see the slightly sharper teeth of the predator.

"Wolf," he confirmed. "We were sent to make sure you were okay. *You* specifically, Maria. Once we realized your home was on the path these cretins were taking, we feared they might be targeting you."

"But why? I'm not a threat to anyone."

Jesse paused beside the unconscious man, kicking his remaining weapons away. Certain he was out cold, Jesse knelt and lifted the man's hand, displaying his wrist for Maria's inspection.

"Do you see anything here? A tattoo maybe?"

"Well, yeah. Of course. Don't you?" She sounded puzzled.

Jesse flipped the man's hand over and took a good long look before dropping it to the ground.

"Nope. Your cousin Sally can see it too. Looks like the magic blood runs true. Both of you can see the mark of the *Venifucus*."

"*Venifucus?*" Maria's tone turned to curiosity as she repeated the unfamiliar word. While she may know the smell of *were* when prompted, it was pretty clear she didn't know much about their greatest enemy. "And you think I have a cousin named Sally? I'm sorry, but I don't think so."

"You do. You just didn't know it. She didn't know about you either until about three weeks ago. She's been searching for you ever since. She located a record of your address earlier today and passed the information along to me. She sensed you might be in danger." He looked around at the demolished kitchen. "Looks like she was right. You can consider me and the guys your personal cavalry." He shrugged. "Although it looks like you had things under control when we got here. So we'll just do the mop up, okay?"

"What are you going to do with them?" She jerked her chin toward the drugged man who was being trussed up by Arlo as they spoke.

"That's for the Alpha to decide."

"You're not the Alpha?" Her tone said she was truly surprised. Jesse flinched a bit at the question. By rights, he should have taken the responsibility instead of leaving it to his younger brother, Jason. But there were things in his past that prevented him from committing fully to Pack life. He'd seen too much. Done too much in wars too far away. It would take time to heal.

He was an Alpha wolf. Always had been. Always would be. He just wasn't *the* Alpha in charge of the Pack. He lived on the outskirts of the Pack and left the running of it to Jason, who hadn't been through the hell Jesse had. Jason was more stable. Better for the Pack. Jesse knew he could best serve the Pack by leaving the leadership of it to Jason.

"I'm *an* Alpha. *The* Alpha is my brother." He didn't go into the details with her. Not yet. Maybe not ever. It was too personal. "The only Pack I'm fit to lead is this small group right here. We few, we happy few, we band of brothers." He turned the small revelation into a joke. Arlo and Len chuckled as they carted the two trussed-up hunters out the kitchen door slung over their shoulders.

"Fancy that. A werewolf who quotes *Henry the Fifth.* I'm impressed." She leaned back against the kitchen counter, more at ease now that it was just the two of them in the house.

"Known a lot of werewolves in your time?"

"None, actually. You're my first." The mischievous smile she gave him made parts of him stand up and take notice of just how scantily clad she really was. He could see the hard tips of her nipples poking at the satin cups of the gown she wore. It only came to mid-thigh, and he had to admire the mile-long shapely legs that were showcased so nicely by the lace trim at the bottom of the hem.

"Then how do you know about us? How did you know what I am?"

"It's the scent of your magic. It's very distinctive. *Were* magic smells kind of wild and golden green."

"You smell in color?" Jesse leaned one hip against the kitchen table, truly interested in everything this alluring woman had to say.

She chuckled at his question. "I never thought of it that way. It's just that *were* magic smells sort of piney. It's faint, but it's like the forest."

"You have to have known at least one *were* to know the scent of our magic. What kind was it?"

"I was friends with a werecougar for a while. Look—" she

shifted as if she were suddenly uncomfortable with how much she had revealed, "—who exactly are you?"

"Major Jesse Moore, US Army, retired. Brother of the Alpha of a large wolf Pack based in Wyoming. Oh, and I should probably mention that my brother just married your cousin, so I guess that makes us related somehow."

"I still don't understand who this supposed long-lost cousin is. You won't be insulted if I don't take everything you tell me at face value. I mean, you did break into my house, after all." Her raised eyebrow challenged him. He liked her spirit.

"Yeah. Sorry about that." He looked once again at the broken back door. "Why don't I put you up for the night at the hotel by the interstate? It would be safer than here, now that we know they know where you are."

"I told you I'm not going anywhere. With you. With those guys. With anyone. My work is here. The animals need me."

"Animals?" Damn. He really wished he'd had more intel about this situation going in. The information Sally had been able to dig up on her cousin was sketchy at best. Just a name and address. Nothing about her occupation or background.

"I'm a veterinarian."

"Seriously?" That was something he hadn't expected.

"I specialize in exotics. Big cats mostly, nowadays."

"Since the run-in with your friend, the werecougar?"

Her head tilted. "Something like that. She said I had a way with felines."

"Really? Sally is at least part wolf, which means you might be too. Cats and dogs usually don't get along."

"The werecougar I knew said I smelled of magic, but she couldn't tell me what kind." Maria looked interested now. There was no way she could hide it, though it was obvious how hard she tried to sound casual.

"This is all tied up with why your cousin was trying to find you, but I can tell you some of it. Sally recently found out she is the descendant of a dryad named Leonora, who lives on Pack lands. Sally is able to pull up a magical family tree of sorts and it shows that she is descended from Leonora's daughter Marisol and a famous werewolf of old. I don't know exactly where you fit on the family tree, but you are a cousin somehow. Whether you come from the wolf line or not, you definitely have dryad magic in you from Leonora."

"If what you're saying is true, it would explain a few things." She looked pensive.

"Is she coming with or staying?" Arlo's voice intruded in Jesse's ear, over the tac radio. Jesse almost jumped. He'd just about forgotten they were in the middle of a mission. Damn. This woman was a killer to his concentration.

"Will advise. Stand by," he answered back, tapping his ear to let Maria know he wasn't talking to her. "The boys want to know if you're staying or going."

"Staying," she said firmly.

"Sure I can't talk you into leaving? It'd be safer. And easier for me to keep you that way."

"I'm not convinced of that. Besides, I haven't made arrangements for anyone else to take care of the animals. I can't leave them in the lurch. The animals in my barns are very ill. I take on the hard cases—those that require surgery or extensive medical treatment—and rehabilitate them to the point where another facility can take them."

They hadn't had time to scout the barns and paddocks. They'd come directly to the house, expecting to have time to work their way outward from there once they'd established that Maria was safe—preferably sleeping peacefully. Only it hadn't turned out that way. They'd arrived, heard the crashing sounds from the kitchen and had to dive right in. Not the best situation ever, but he'd dealt with worse in his time.

"All right." He looked out the window and noticed the slight pinkening of the eastern horizon. "It's nearly dawn. I'll send the guys back with the prisoners for my brother to deal with. If you'll allow, I'll stay here and repair the damage our entry caused to your home. I'd also like to arrange for you to speak with your cousin. Maybe she can explain in more detail and convince you to help."

"Help? Who, exactly, needs my help?"

Jesse sighed. It really was too complex to bombard the woman with all this at once.

"Leonora. She's in a sort of suspended animation inside a willow tree. Damndest thing I ever saw, and that's saying something. The two men who attacked you tonight? One of their friends shot Leonora with a poisonous silver bullet during the dust up in Wyoming three weeks ago. Before going into the willow, she made Sally promise to find her long-lost family and gather them together to help her. Only together can you save her life, she said."

"So now you're telling me someone's life is in danger and only I—and some alleged family members I've never even heard of—can save her?"

"I know it's a lot to take in."

"No shit." Her muttered profanity made him smile. Damn, he liked this woman.

"How about we take this one step at a time?" He tried to sound less threatening and more warm and fuzzy. Not so easy when you had an assault weapon strapped across your chest, but he'd give it his best shot. "We'll secure the perimeter and then I'll send the guys on their way. I can fix up your door and any other damage today. I can even help you around the farm. Consider me your personal slave for the day. It's the least I can do to make up for smashing in here. Then maybe this afternoon you can talk to Sally and learn more about what's going on back home. What do you say?"

She stared at him for a long moment, narrowing her eyes and tilting her head in the most adorable manner as she considered. He wasn't sure she was going to go for Plan B. It would've been so much easier if she'd just gone along with Plan A and come quietly. Now he had to improvise, and his Plan C was cloudy at best. Plan C covered what to do if she turned down Plan B, and it wasn't ideal. Not at all.

Come on, baby. Go with Plan B.

"All right."

Jessie tried not to let his sigh of relief come out too loudly.

"You—" she pointed at him, "—I want you outside with your men. I'm going upstairs to get dressed. Might as well start the day. I'd have been up in a half hour anyway. Secure your perimeter, whatever that means, but stay the hell away from the white barn. If the cats in there smell werewolf, it might upset them. It's hard to predict how they'll react, and I don't want to deal with a half dozen frenzied felines."

"You might be surprised. They tell me I have a way with pussy...cats." He couldn't help himself. The woman begged to be teased what with the way her thin satin nightie teased him. He was hard just from looking at her long legs under the lace-trimmed satin.

"Behave, wolfman," she threw over her shoulder as she headed out of the kitchen. "I'll meet you by the back door in fifteen minutes."

Jesse met his men on the back porch and handed out orders as they marched toward one of the vehicles they'd stashed down the road out of sight. The back of the pickup truck would do well for prisoner transport. What happened to the two men after they got them back to Wyoming was up to Jason. He was the Alpha, after all. Jesse had to remind himself of that occasionally, but the arrangement worked for the most part. Jason gave Jesse complete autonomy over the Pack's small but growing contingent of former professional soldiers— now tasked with keeping the Pack safe when not on outside assignment.

Jesse had built an elite clientele among the various shifter Tribes, Packs and Clans. When something of a paramilitary nature needed to be done, he and his select group were the ones called upon to do it. They hadn't been in business long, but they had quickly gained a reputation for getting the job done.

Securing the prisoners in the bed of the pickup truck, Arlo and Jesse split up to scout the perimeter. Len was left to guard the prisoners and act as home base, should they run into trouble. It wasn't likely, but it was best to be prepared for all possibilities. Arlo and Jesse each went in a separate direction. They met in the middle on the other side of the house. Their paths had taken them past the three barns and into some of the open pasture. Jesse scented the big cats, along with a few other varieties of animals. It would be interesting to see how Maria interacted with some of the creatures she had on her property.

Considering the fact that she refused to leave, Jesse figured he'd have his chance to do just that later in the day. But first he had to get his men on their way. He gave Arlo the high sign as they passed each other and continued on the circuit, moving in a bit from the sector they'd already checked. By the time they circled back to the truck, the full perimeter had been scouted. No big surprises. The two hunters had approached on a pretty straightforward vector. Jesse had sniffed it out almost immediately once he got near the driveway.

The hunters weren't very crafty when it came to hiding their presence. They'd taken only minimum precautions, which spoke of lack of skill and just plain sloppiness. Jesse wasn't impressed.

"These guys must be the B Team," he observed when he reached Len. "They came in on the side of the driveway. Their vehicle is stashed in those bushes up at the road, right next to the entrance to Maria's land. Take it with you when you go."

"You're not coming?" Arlo asked, joining them as he completed his circuit of the perimeter.

"She refused to leave. She's a veterinarian with a lot of sick animals that only she can take care of, supposedly. I'm going to stay and convince her otherwise. Help her find someone to fill in with the beasties."

"I thought I smelled lioness, but I figured I had to be wrong." Arlo shook his head.

"Nope. Your sniffer is good. Lions, tigers and probably bears too, for that matter. Our little Maria is a brave one."

"Don't like leaving you here alone, Jess." Arlo was one of Jesse's closest and oldest friends. His expression was troubled.

"Yeah, I feel it too." They both had a sixth sense for impending danger. "It's why I'm staying. She refuses to leave, and if these guys found her, you know their bosses have to be on their way."

"If this was the B Team, the A Team could be right behind them," Len observed in his quiet way. Len was usually a man of few words. That he chose to speak now indicated he felt the same danger in the air. Not good. But what could Jesse do?

"And we can't risk keeping these guys here. I want Jason to have a chance to question them. Maybe send them on to the Lords if necessary, so the priestesses can have a crack at them. Either way, these two could have information, and I want to give my brother every chance to extract it. Low-level guys like these won't have the same protections against spilling their secrets as the higher-ups. They probably don't know as much, but what they do know is easier to get at."

Arlo and Len were both nodding. They knew full well what was at stake. The safety of their Pack and perhaps all shifters who fought on the side of Light. "Get them back to Jason as quick as you can. I'll stay in touch by phone. We'll plan as we go if the situation here goes south."

"I don't like it, but I guess it's what we've got," Arlo ground out.

"I hear you, brother."

Chapter Two

It had been a bitch of a morning. Maria cursed under her breath as she yanked on her underwear and jeans. She then threw on an old shirt with angry movements. First, the noise of an intruder had awoken her and then two guys had attacked her when she went to investigate.

She never locked her back door. The oaf who had broken in after she'd already subdued the intruders could have spared himself the trouble if he'd just tried the knob. Like the first set of burglars had.

Part of the reason she didn't lock her door was that people sometimes brought injured animals to her at all hours of the day and night. It simplified matters if they could get inside easily. Most people in these parts were honest and the crime rate was incredibly low. She'd never had a problem before.

All that changed when not one, but two sets of asshats decided to rumble through her kitchen in the dark hours before dawn. She didn't really know what to believe, but she wanted to give the guy who had remained behind a chance to prove himself. He'd taken away the first set of idiots and sent his men away as well. That had to count for something.

Or maybe he was just playing her. Trying to lull her into a sense of security before attempting what the first two idiots had—abduction. No way was she going anywhere with anyone. Not now. Possibly not ever.

She would have called the cops if she thought they'd actually do something. But her sanctuary wasn't popular, and she was already *persona non grata* with the local sheriff. Her immediate neighbors didn't like the idea of wild animals so nearby and had sent the sheriff over to read her the riot act more than once. She didn't like the man and it was clear the feelings were mutual. After their previous confrontations, she knew he wouldn't spit on her if she was on fire.

She would fight whatever battle might come on her own land, and on her own terms. She'd fought too long and too hard to create this little oasis of calm in an otherwise turbulent world. She needed the peace she found here, on her sanctuary, away from other people and surrounded by her animal friends.

This place was a balm to her soul and she wouldn't give it up easily.

But there was something about the hottie who'd broken through her kitchen door as if it had been made of paper. His strength impressed her, but there was also something in his eyes. It was a wounded wariness she often saw in the eyes of the animals that came to her for healing. And he wasn't hard to look at either. In fact, he was just about the yummiest thing that had walked across her path in too many days to count. Years, even.

Yes, sir, when the good Lord was handing out handsome, that boy got a double helping. And he didn't carry himself as if he either knew it, or cared. She liked that about him too.

She didn't really know the first thing about him, yet something inside her stood up and took notice when his gravelly voice rasped over her senses. Yeah, she liked the way his simplest words caressed her nerve endings and even the way his gaze had roamed over her body in obvious appreciation. She'd give him a chance to prove himself either way. The animals should do it. They'd give her a clue as to his inner character. They were the most objective judges of character she'd ever known and she trusted them as she trusted no other.

"Time to face the music," she said to herself as she opened her bedroom door and headed down the stairs to meet him. It was time to feed the menagerie.

Maria found him at the kitchen door, his weapons placed carefully beside him as he examined the damage he'd done to the frame and knob. He'd already removed some of the dangling hardware and the largest of the splinters. At least he appeared to be making good on his promise to fix her door. He'd broken it, after all.

"I'm going to need to replace a bit of the trim and this wood right here." He pointed to a section that had been mostly demolished by his entry. "I don't suppose you have anything like this on hand?" His gaze met hers with a skeptical tilt of his head.

She hadn't made much noise as she entered the kitchen, but he'd known she was there. He definitely had sharper senses than the average person. It would be interesting to learn the extent of his werewolf talents.

"There might be something out in the red barn. The previous owners had a lot of lumber scraps that I kept. Sometimes I use bits of them to cobble together things I need for the animals." She moved into the room and toward the door, grabbing her jacket from the hook on the wall as she went. "Speaking of which, I need to go check on everyone and do the morning feed."

He didn't even have to be asked. He stood, throwing his assault rifle casually over one shoulder. The strap that held it looked well worn, and he carried the giant gun as if it belonged there. As if he always went about heavily armed. Like a soldier who had seen more than his fair share of action in dangerous places.

"So what do I call you? Major? Major Moore? Jesse?" she asked as they left the kitchen through the broken door. He took a moment to secure it as best he could.

"Jesse's good." Apparently he was a man of few words.

"I'm Doctor Maria Garibaldi, as you no doubt already

know." They walked quickly through the brisk morning air.

The sun was up and the day beginning to warm, but there were still sparkling droplets of dew in the grass and on the leaves. It was a magical time of morning that Maria usually enjoyed in solitude, listening to the whispering song of the leaves and grass.

"*Doctor* Garibaldi," he spoke her name in a respectful tone, emphasizing her title. "Our intel didn't include that little fact. We were operating on very little information, but I'm glad we arrived when we did."

She decided to give him a little credit. "Me too. Not that I wasn't already handling the situation, but I'd rather not involve the local sheriff in anything I don't have to."

"Why's that?" He looked at her sharply, and she instantly regretted her words. She probably shouldn't have mentioned her problems with local law enforcement to this guy she barely knew. Too late now.

"Let's just say, a few folks weren't very happy when I set up my shingle here. One or two of the local landowners objected strongly to the idea of a wildlife sanctuary in their midst, and the local sheriff...well... It might be too much to say that he tried to run me off, but it sure felt that way for a while. I'd rather not let him know that I had trouble here. It would only add fuel to the fire of those who want me gone."

"I'm sorry," Jessie replied. As if he had any control over the local biases. "We shifters tend to handle things ourselves and keep human law enforcement out of it as much as possible, so you're in the clear as far as I'm concerned. If you continue to have problems with the sheriff, I'd be willing to have a few words with him if you like. I'm not sure what I can do, but I'd be willing to try."

"While I appreciate the offer, I've learned it's best not to have any dealings with the man that aren't strictly necessary. He's a real jerk."

"Sorry to hear that." Again, his concern seemed real. "Sally is a former police detective. She used to live and work in San Francisco before meeting my little brother and moving out to Wyoming to live. She might have some pull. She gets along well with other cops from what I've seen."

"This is my supposed long-lost cousin you're talking about, right? She's a werewolf?"

"No," Jesse was quick to clarify. "In fact, before coming to Wyoming, she had no knowledge of the existence of Others. Although, far back in her ancestry—and yours too—is a very powerful dryad. Sally has a little bit of wolf blood, but she can't shift. She can do things with plants and trees though that would amaze you."

"Maybe not as much as you think," she mumbled as they approached the first outbuilding. "Are you still willing to help with the feed?" She turned to him as she slid open the oversized door.

He smiled at her and her heart literally skipped a beat. Damn. He really was too handsome for his own good.

"I'm happy to help."

"Good." She cleared her throat, trying to regain some of her usual equilibrium. "Take out the plastic bag full of red meat from the refrigerator and set it on the table." She nodded toward the work island in the center of the kitchen area.

There were a couple of freezers and one big industrial refrigerator on the perimeter of the area. There was also ample counter space and some very large knives in a wooden block on the counter by the sink. The cabinets were full of the tools of her trade—medicines and supplies to help her treat her furry patients.

Maria opened the medicine cabinet and took out what she needed. She used a mix of her own healing energy and manmade drugs to help her patients. There were too many for her to heal all by herself. If she tried—as she had when she was a youngster—she would be knocked unconscious from the strain. She'd learned through trial and a lot of error that she gave of her own energy when she healed and a complex or prolonged healing could push her to dangerously low levels.

So she'd decided long ago on a compromise. She'd gone to veterinary school and gotten all the knowledge and credentials she needed. That, combined with her innate abilities, had made her a much more successful vet than most.

Jesse sniffed as she neared, holding a few of the pills she meant to incorporate into some of her patients' meat.

"Oral antibiotics?"

"You can smell that?" She set the paper cup that held the pills on the table near the bag of meat he'd retrieved.

"Yep. My sniffer is very sensitive." His lips quirked in a small grin that was altogether too charming. She had to be on her toes with this guy. He could too easily trick her into liking him.

"Interesting," was her only comment. Frankly, she didn't know what to say to that.

The idea that he could shift form into a giant wolf made her knees weak. She'd met only one shifter, and that one had been female and young. The werecougar woman hadn't been all that intimidating when she was in her feline form, and when she was human she was frail as a willow.

This guy was the most imposing man she'd ever seen up close. His size was on the enormous scale and his muscles had muscles. If he ever did turn into a wolf in her presence, she'd probably wet her pants.

Maria went about her work silently, inserting the pills into flaps she cut in the meat. It wasn't the most efficient way of delivering the drugs, but it would have to do for now. She didn't want to take too many chances with her newest guest, a young bear with a badly infected gunshot wound. He'd been anesthetized when he came in, courtesy of a friendly animal control officer, and she'd been able to dig out the bullet and stitch him up while he was still out.

She'd also been able to administer antibiotics and other medicines by injection while he was safely unconscious. Now, however, he was up and about. Even in pain, he was really not happy about being caged. He attacked the bars and paced every time she entered the barn, watching her with an angry expression. She tried not to take it personally, but she was still kind of surprised by his violent reaction. He really was a wild one and refused to let her near. She didn't want to tranquilize him any more than necessary.

Maria placed the spiked meat back on the tray and went to get a few pounds of chicken she'd had thawing in the refrigerator. She used this building as her surgery and prep room. The barns were where she kept her larger patients while they recovered. It was easier and more secure, also quieter for the animals farther away from the house and the driveway.

She prepared the chicken and some more beef for the cats, adding portions to another tray. When she was done, she loaded Jesse with the larger tray and picked up the smaller one herself. Might as well take advantage of having him around while he was here. They walked toward the first barn, which was full of cats. She could hear the uproar already as they neared.

"They smell me." Jesse stopped short of the door. "Maybe I'd better wait outside or they'll never settle down."

Maria listened to the unusual ruckus inside and hastily agreed. "I'll be right back."

She took the larger tray from him and left him with the smaller one, rushing into the barn and making her rounds quickly. The patients were all doing well, if agitated by the werewolf scent outside. They quieted down when they got their meals and Jesse didn't come any closer.

Rejoining him outside the door, she smiled tentatively and

pointed to the tray he still held.

"This is for the new bear. He's in the next building." She led the way, chattering a bit to cover her surprise at the cats' reactions. "He's a juvenile and not happy about being here. Hopefully he'll take the pills this way. If he doesn't, I'll have to try something else."

"What's wrong with him?"

"He was shot a few days ago. Animal control tranq'ed him and brought him to me when he strayed too close to somebody's house. I took the bullet out and stitched him up. He was unconscious most of the first day. Yesterday, he was back to his ornery self. Nearly ripped my hand off when I strayed too close to his cage, but he needs more antibiotics. His wound was already infected when they brought him to me."

"What kind of bear?"

"Grizzly," she answered as she opened the barn door. She noticed when Jesse's head came up suddenly, his eyes peering intently into the darkness beyond the door.

"He's more than that." Jesse put the tray down on the table just inside the door and went inside ahead of her. "Stay back, Doc. Let me talk to him."

"Oh, Lord. Do you mean to say I've got another shifter in a cage? Crap!" She was upset. More than upset, to be honest. She knew about shifters now. They were people, not just animals. They didn't need—or deserve—to be caged. "No wonder he's not happy with me."

She tried to push in front of Jesse, but he wouldn't budge. He approached the cage and stared down at the small bear inside. Jesse cursed under his breath and crouched down, way too close to the bars had this been a truly wild animal.

"Hey, sport," he greeted the youngster. "You're safe. You can shift now. The doc didn't know you were *were*, but she knows about us and she's safe. Are you well enough to take your skin and talk to me? Tell me where your parents are and

I'll get them. They must be worried sick."

The bear only growled, in obvious pain as it lay panting on the floor. It glared at Maria over Jesse's shoulder.

"I'm so sorry," she tried. "I didn't know you were a shifter. I've only met one before. If I'd known, I would've done this differently. I'm really, really sorry."

The bear sniffed in her direction, then focused his nose and his gaze on the werewolf in front of her.

"She's on the level." Jesse looked at the lock holding the cage closed. "You lock them in, Doc?" His tone was full of condemnation, and she felt just awful, but she had her reasons.

"It's to protect them. I had problems once before with someone trying to steal the animals in the middle of the night. Some of my patients are worth a lot of money on the exotic-animal black market." She reached into her pocket and produced the key, handing it to Jesse.

"If you use simple latches, we can shift form and let ourselves out if we get caught in our fur by mistake. Of course, a full-grown grizzly shifter could probably break this little lock, no problem, but an injured youngster? No wonder he's mad at you."

"I'm so sorry," she repeated herself, but she couldn't help it. She felt like a villain. Lower than pond scum. She inhaled and realized there was the faint scent of magical shifter pine around the bear, but it was so obscured by the other scents that she wasn't too surprised she'd missed it.

Jesse unlocked the small metal fastener and unlatched the cage.

"Stand back, Doc, just in case he's not quite with us. Pain and fever tend to bring out our wild sides."

Taking his advice, Maria retreated a few steps. The young bear lurched to his feet and growled. Jesse reached right into the cage and held his hand out to the bear, daring greatly, in Maria's opinion.

"Come on, sport. I'm not the enemy. Your people and mine have been allied for centuries. I'll help you, if I can." The bear swiped at the back of Jesse's hand with his tongue. Maria gasped when she saw its mouth open and then sighed when she realized it was tasting Jesse, not biting him. "Who shot you, son?" Jesse's voice crooned, speaking to calm the young bear. "I'm Major Jesse Moore. My brother, Jason, is the Alpha of the Wyoming wolf Pack. I was Special Forces and I came here tracking *Venifucus* agents who kidnapped a wolf child last week. We got him back. We took care of him—a young boy maybe just a bit younger than you. They kidnapped him and strapped a bomb to his chest, but we rescued him and he's fine now, back with his parents. Me and my men—that's what we do. We protect the Pack and other shifters. Anyone on the side of Light who needs us. And we'll help you too, young bear of the Grizzly Clan. You have my word on it."

The bear went still, seeming to measure Jesse's words. Maria didn't realize she was holding her breath until the bear nodded slightly, moving forward, out of the cage.

"How do you want to do this, sport?" Jesse was still talking to the bear who moved beside him. "If it was me, I'd want someplace soft to land when I retook my skin. How about we find you a bed where you can recuperate in more civilized style?" Jesse's teasing grin seemed to catch the bear's attention. It moved its head up and down, as if nodding agreement. Jesse turned to her. "How about your guest room? When he shifts, he's going to be naked and weak. It'd be easier to let him shift on or near the bed."

On the one hand, Maria felt terribly guilty to have caged a shifter. Of course, she only had this man's words—and the actions of the young bear—to convince her the grizzly actually could take human form. All the evidence pointed toward the bear being one of those rare, magical beings who could shapeshift, and Maria would be worse than negligent to make the youngster stay in the barn if he really was what she now believed he was.

Mind made up, she led the way toward the door, even if she was a little uneasy at the thought of a bear entering her home. He'd be human soon enough, or so she believed. She hoped she was right about this. Otherwise, if this was some kind of practical joke, Jesse Moore was going to be so dead, he wouldn't know what hit him, Special Forces or not.

As she passed the tray by the door, she paused. "Um...what about the meat?"

Jesse was about ten feet behind her with the slow-moving bear. The young grizzly was sort of hopping on two hind feet and only one front paw, holding the other paw to his chest, clearly in pain. Jesse shrugged, strode forward and grabbed the tray. Then he turned back to the bear.

"Do you want any of this?" he asked the bear point blank.

The juvenile sniffed at the tray and then shook his head. At that point, Maria knew for certain this was no ordinary bear.

"I didn't think so." Jesse walked over to her and handed the tray to her. "Maybe you can salvage some of this for your other patients. The antibiotics give the meat a funny smell. I can see why he wouldn't trust you enough right now to eat it. Shifters have learned to be very cautious when dealing with regular humans."

"I'm so sorry," she said again, feeling it down to her bones. She couldn't imagine what horrible things had been done to shifters by regular folk who thought they were just animals. Being locked up. Hunted. Tranquilized. Just as the grizzly had been when it arrived on her doorstep. She turned and fled toward the house, carrying the tray.

She looked back over her shoulder just once, to realize why Jesse had wanted both hands free. His gun was slung across his body, the strap making a diagonal line across his impressive chest while the black metal of the firearm rested across his back. He crouched low at the bear's side, offering it support and helping it cross the distance between the barn and the house. She couldn't hear the words he spoke to the youngster, but she saw his lips moving and sensed he offered encouragement and perhaps some comfort to the creature. She turned back to the house, knowing the young male was in good hands.

She threw open the broken back door to the kitchen and deposited the meat on the counter on her way through toward the guest room on the first floor. She'd converted the small room to a bedroom when her grandmother had come to stay for a while. It had been easier to let the old woman sleep on the first floor than to subject the poor dear to the stairs.

Maria was glad of it now as she stripped the flowered bedspread from the twin mattress. It had clean white sheets and good pillows. Aside from the rather feminine, flowery wall paper and furnishings, the young man she expected the bear to become would be comfortable. He'd even have his own small bathroom just off the kitchen and easy access to the refrigerator once he was up and around.

She heard the unmistakable click of claws on the kitchen linoleum. Taking a deep breath for courage, she stood her ground at the side of the bed, waiting for Jesse and his bear friend to enter the small room.

The bear entered first, looking around and then settling his gaze on her. She gulped, unable to hide a little tremor at the condemnation she read in his dark eyes.

Rather than apologize again, she stepped away from the bed, which was placed in the center of the room. The bear limped painfully over to the other side of the bed and stopped, turning his back to her.

"Do you want me to leave?" she asked Jesse as he filled the doorway.

"Shifters aren't usually shy." His lips quirked in a grin that made her hot just thinking what he might not be shy about. "It's up to him, but it'd be good to have you here in case he starts to bleed when he goes human. These bodies are more fragile in many ways than our furry counterparts. But sometimes the magic of shifting itself helps heal things that otherwise would take much longer, and grizzlies are said to be among the most magical of our kind. So it's show time, sport," Jesse addressed the young bear. "Show us what you got."

Maria felt a tingle against her skin, almost like a static charge all over her body. *Magic,* she thought. She'd felt that sensation only a few times before in her life, when her nona did her magic. Maria's breath caught as the bear's body began to elongate within a shimmering golden-brown mist. A moment later, the bear was gone and a young man stood in his place.

A very naked and battered young man. And he was bleeding.

"Oh, crap," the boy said as he slid toward the bed, falling into unconsciousness. Jesse was there to catch him even as Maria jumped forward. He laid the kid gently on the bed and covered him with the sheet.

"Damn," Jesse said softly. "This guy's been through the wringer. We should probably redress the wound while he's out. Shifters don't handle pain medication well. The normal doses for humans aren't strong enough, so to get any kind of numbing effect, we need dangerously high doses. Alcohol is the usual anesthetic of choice, but this one is a little too young and in too bad shape to risk getting him drunk."

"Agreed." Maria sprang into action, going to the nearby hall closet to get supplies. "Could you run some warm water? There's a basin on the shelf in there."

While she was in the hall, she heard the water in the bathroom sink running, though she hadn't heard Jesse move past her to get into the tiny bathroom. The man moved like a wraith.

When she went back into the room a moment later, Jesse was already there, cleaning the area around the wound in the young man's chest with a wet washcloth. It was clear he knew what to do.

"Seen a lot of gunshot wounds in your line of work?" she asked, only half joking.

"Too many," he answered in a tone that made her smile go away. He wasn't kidding around. It had been insensitive of her to try to make light of something so serious. Seemed like she was screwing up left and right with these people.

"Sorry," she mumbled, concentrating on her work.

When the kid had been in bear form, she was in her element. She'd taken the bullet out, stitched him up and not thought twice about it. But when faced with a human patient, she was feeling a lot less sure of herself. Thankfully, the surgery had already been done.

"Are things in the same place, more or less from one form to another?" she had to ask. The ramifications of her surgery were just now occurring to her.

"Mostly. I'm more familiar with wolves, you understand," Jesse answered as he kept working, very efficient in his movements so he didn't jar the patient. "What did you diagnose when he was a bear?"

"The bullet came very close to his lung, but luckily it didn't penetrate. I believe it glanced off a rib and that caused it to stop short of causing more serious injury. Not that this isn't serious." She examined the wound closely. What she saw brought her up short. "This is far more healed than it should be."

"Shifting can sometimes speed things up a bit," Jesse said nonchalantly. Maria was impressed. The wound was nearly sealed. It was still an angry red, but the sutures she'd put in weren't really necessary anymore. He was bleeding from a new tear near the suture line, probably made while walking here. Even as she watched, the bleeding slowed and finally stopped.

"I used dissolving sutures, but I think I should take these

out." She bathed the wound thoroughly, clearing away old blood and revealing the much-improved wound.

"Do that now, while he's still out. He doesn't need the stitches anymore. They're only getting in the way of his natural healing."

"Good point." Maria got out the supplies she'd need to pick out the stitches.

"What about his arm? This looks like it was pretty deep." Jesse had continued working, checking all the obvious wounds.

"I had some butterfly bandages on that. I guess they must've come off when he changed." She reached into the first aid kit she'd brought in from the hall closet. "It's okay. I have more."

They worked together. Jesse bathed the gash on the youngster's arm, quietly cleaning and disinfecting the deep red slash. It looked like a knife cut to Maria. She watched Jesse's work while she snipped and pulled on the stitches.

"I can't figure why the bullet hole improved when he shifted, but the arm injury didn't. It was the less serious of the two wounds," she observed.

Jesse's face was grim when she looked up at him.

"I think I know why." Jesse didn't elaborate but set about slathering the cut with antibiotic gel he found in her emergency kit, then he expertly used the butterflies to close it up again. "Do you have a blood pressure cuff?"

"Hang on." She rummaged around in the night stand. Her grandmother had one of those wrist devices her doctor had suggested that she never used. Maria had seen it in here the last time she'd cleaned the room. She flipped open the protective plastic case and checked the batteries before placing the small device on the young man's wrist. As they waited for the machine to register, she tried to think about what she'd done for the bear when he'd arrived.

"He'd lost a lot of blood when he got here," she told Jesse. "I

35

gave him a unit of saline and he stabilized.

"Our human forms can often be more delicate than our animals."

The cuff beeped and Maria bent to look at the results. "Not good."

"He needs a drip."

Maria was surprised by Jesse's knowledge. "I've never worked on a human being before." She paused by the door, already thinking where her closest supplies were and how to get everything they needed as quickly as possible.

"It's okay. I have. We do all kinds of advanced first aid in the service. Special Forces learns more than most."

His confidence made her feel a lot better as she scrambled for supplies. Luckily, she had what they needed here in the house and didn't have to run to any of the outbuildings. She was back in less than a minute, glad to see Jesse had already made preparations.

He took the I.V. kit from her and tore it open, leaving her in no doubt as to his familiarity with the equipment. He placed the needle expertly as she set up the drip. Within moments, life-sustaining fluid was flowing into their patient's veins, helping his depleted body stabilize. Maria kept monitoring his blood pressure and other vital signs, glad when they started to improve.

"I think he's out of the woods," Maria said softly, glad for the slight ease in tension gained from knowing the young man wasn't going to die on her just yet.

A few minutes later, the kid started coming around. Jesse encouraged him by talking to him and reassuring him. All in all, Jesse impressed the heck out of her. He could be gentle when he wanted to be and didn't mind letting it show, which said something very significant to her about his character.

Oh, yes. She could grow to like him all too easily. Actually, she was afraid she already had. Darn it.

Chapter Three

"Come on, sport. Can you tell me your name?" Jesse asked one more time.

"Zach," came the weak reply. The kid was getting stronger by the moment, but he wasn't quite back with them yet.

"Zach. That's good. What's your last name?" Jesse encouraged.

Dark-brown eyes shot open defiantly. "Smith," he enunciated with a bit of fire.

Jesse laughed. The kid had spirit. He wasn't trusting them with his real name. At least not his surname, which would help them trace his family. Smart kid. He'd come under fire and, if Jesse didn't miss his guess, attack by poisonous silver, which meant whoever had come after him knew what he was. The kid had been shot, poisoned and captured, but he still did what he could to protect his family.

"That's all right, Zach. I'll do what I can to reassure you that we're the good guys. Even if the doc didn't know what you were at first."

He saw the woman cringe out of the corner of his eye. She'd been apologizing a lot, and he didn't mean to make her feel worse, but the kid needed to be convinced first, then they could work on the rest of this situation. The presence of the werebear and the nature of his injuries made him wonder if those two cretins last night had been after the doc...or the bear. Either was possible. One thing he knew for sure, this situation had just become a whole lot more complicated.

Even more complicated than when he'd gotten his first good whiff of her alluring scent. He'd known from that moment this mission was going to test him in ways he'd never been tested before.

He'd wanted to wrap his arms around her and kiss her senseless. He'd wanted to seduce her and bend her over the kitchen table, flip up that slinky nightie and fuck her brains out. Then do it all again. But he'd refrained. He'd kept his mind on the mission even if the wood in his pants made it hard to walk.

He'd been the model of restraint—half-convincing himself that once he got her back to Wyoming he'd have his chance to woo and ultimately claim her the way his inner wolf was howling to do. He'd been all set to do his very best sales patter on how her cousin and ancestor needed her while he helped her with the wild animals she cared for. Then he'd discovered an even bigger problem under her roof.

No longer was his mission only about Maria Garibaldi. It now had to include the nearly helpless bear shifter who didn't trust him worth a damn. Not that Jesse blamed the kid. He'd been through hell. No doubt about it. He was wise to be cautious with strangers, even if one was a fellow shifter. Shifters had gone bad and betrayed their own kind before. Not often, but it had been known to happen.

"All right, sport." Jesse patted the kid's uninjured arm. "I'm going to make some calls. My brother will be able to get a priority message to the Lords and I might be able to rig some kind of internet call or something so you can see for yourself which side I'm on. Will you give me the chance to do that? I'd hate to have to follow your ass out the window and track you to where you drop from your injuries. In case you didn't realize it, you've been poisoned. That isn't going to go away easily or quickly."

The young man glanced down at his arm and Jesse knew he understood. Zach had been sliced with a silver blade. Poisoned as well as injured. All shifters knew the danger of silver.

"I'll stay for a while. More than that, I can't promise."

"Good man." Jesse nodded approvingly.

"But I don't want her in here, or I swear I'll bite her." The kid glared at Maria and she gasped, tears filling her eyes as she fled the room.

Damn. Rage filled Jesse as he watched Maria's cute tail scurry out the door. He understood the guilt she was feeling. The kid's anger didn't help matters.

"You keep a civil tongue in your head when it comes to the doc, Zach. She didn't know you were a shifter. Even so, she saved your life. She performed surgery on you to remove the bullet and stitched you up the best she knew how. Without her, you'd probably be dead by now, so you thank your lucky stars she was the one animal control brought you to. If you'd fallen to your attackers, you'd be in a lot worse shape by now."

That seemed to stifle the kid for now, but he still looked rebelliously suspicious as he lay in the granny bed and glared at him. Jesse sighed heavily.

"Is there anyone I can call for you? I'll give you my phone to make the call if that helps."

"And then you'll have their numbers and they'll come under fire? No, thank you."

Jesse shook his head. "I understand and applaud your caution, but you're dead wrong here. Give me an hour and I'll prove it."

The stubborn chin nodded. "An hour. Then I'm history."

Jesse knew it wasn't an idle threat. Grizzly shifters were among the most magical. If Zach really wanted to try to evade him, he'd probably manage it. Werebears could hide their trail by magical means so that even other shifters couldn't follow.

Jesse left the room and went in search of Maria. He found her not far away, sitting on the couch in the living room. Her eyes were dry, but she didn't look happy. Still, she was bearing up under the stress better than he'd expected.

"I've got some calls to make. I don't suppose you have videoconferencing capabilities?" he asked, taking a shot in the dark.

"I have a laptop with a camera. You can video chat on it, I think."

"That's better than nothing." Jesse was already dialing as he spoke. Maria bounced up off the couch and left the room.

"Jason, we've got a complication," Jesse said to his brother as soon as he answered the phone.

"What's going on? I got an update from Arlo about twenty minutes ago. The prisoners are secure and on their way here. He said you were having trouble convincing the woman to leave her farm."

Jesse took a split second to marvel again at how well the position of Alpha suited his little brother. He had grown into the responsibility that had been thrust upon him during the chaos after their parents' deaths. Jesse, by rights, should've fought for the position, but after the wars he'd been through, his heart and mind weren't fully with the Pack anymore. Jason had been the one to step up and fight for their birthright. He'd fought off all comers, avenging their parents' deaths and restoring order to the Pack. He'd done well, and Jesse couldn't be more proud of him.

"It's more than that. The lady is a veterinarian. She has a number of exotic and large wild animals on her place. It's a sanctuary."

"Yeah, Arlo told me a bit about it. Can't she get someone to watch over the critters for a bit?"

"It's not that. She had a bear here with a gunshot wound. Jesse, he's a shifter. A grizzly. Shot in the chest and knifed with a silver blade along one arm. He doesn't trust me worth shit right now and I've got one hour to convince him I'm one of the good guys."

"What do you want me to do?" Jason went from casual

questioning to deadly serious from one heartbeat to the next. Damn.

Jesse really liked the fact that he could depend on his little bro as much or even more than any member of his elite team. He led the small group of ex-Special Forces shifters and he'd staked his life on their loyalty time and again. He was coming to learn that Jason was just as reliable and even more resourceful in some ways due to his position as Alpha of one of the most influential Packs in the country.

"Call the Lords. See if they'll do a video chat with the kid. I need him to know I'm on the level, and I need him to tell me where his parents are. I have a bad feeling about the fact that he was out there on his own, shot and damaged enough to be hunted and caught by human animal control officers. He caught a break when they tranq'ed him and brought him to Maria. She performed surgery on his chest and stitched him up, but she caged him, not knowing he was a shifter, and he's understandably pissed." Jesse took a breath, needing to lay it on the line with his brother. "At this point, I'm not even sure if the attack on Maria's house last night was due to her presence or that of the grizzly kid. Could be those hunters were sent to get him and she was just a bonus." He cursed under his breath. "Or it could be the other way around. Until the kid starts talking, I just don't know."

"All right. Get to a computer and stand by. Sign into your account and I'll form the link. We can probably patch the Lords through that way, if they're around. I'll send a priority call as soon as you hang up."

"Then I'm gone. Clock's ticking." Jesse disconnected the call and turned to find Maria standing behind him with a laptop in her hands.

"So you thought those two jerks this morning were after me, but now you're not so sure? They might've been after Zach?" Her hands were shaking, but her spine was firm with the inner strength she'd demonstrated up to this point.

"Sorry you heard that, but yes. That's about the size of it." He stepped toward her and held out his hand. She placed the laptop in his grip after a slight hesitation and he stared into her expressive eyes, caught by the worry in her gaze.

"I can't just let him leave with you and stay behind, can I? They really will come back. Or, if not those two, more like them. Right?"

"Yes, Maria. I'm sorry. By taking Zach in, you've compromised your own safety. Or vice versa. I won't know which until we figure out exactly who they were after. But now that two of their number have been captured and are missing, they'll send more. It might take a day or two before they realize what happened here, but they'll find out and then they'll send a more professional team to handle you."

She took a deep, steadying breath and looked away, thinking hard. When she turned back to him, it seemed she had come to a decision.

"All right. I'm going to call in some backup to watch over the animals. I have a contingency plan for the occasional times I'm sick or need to go someplace. There's a couple that can come by a few times a day to feed and check on the animals. They should be all right since it sounds like the bad guys will probably leave once they realize we're gone. I'll go with you and Zach to Wyoming until all this is sorted out."

Jesse felt relief in his heart unlike any he'd felt before. He'd been tied up in knots about how to get her cooperation, and now he suddenly had it. He should be happy. Instead he felt an urgency to bundle her up and get her out of here as soon as possible. He'd learned not to ignore those kinds of feelings.

"Make the arrangements and then pack a bag. We're going to hit the road as soon as I can convince Zach." Jesse opened the laptop and began firing it up.

"He's not really in condition to travel." She bit her lower lip, probably worrying about her patient.

The unconscious action made Jesse think some very inappropriate thoughts about kissing her worries away and sinking his own teeth into her flesh...in a pleasurable way. Not to hurt. Only to tantalize.

He cleared his throat and tried to focus on her words, not that little bit of pink softness begging to be kissed. He'd wanted to feel her plump, feminine lips under his since almost the first moment he'd seen her kicking ass in her kitchen. In the slinky-as-sin revealing nightie that would star in his dreams for years to come, he was sure.

"He'll have to be ready." Jesse tried to get his thoughts back on track. "We need to get out of here. The three of us will be no match for the next batch of assassins."

"You think they want to kill him?" She seemed really upset by the idea.

"Him. You. Me. The *Venifucus* probably want all of us dead. They—or somebody—already tried to kill Zach once. Those guys in your kitchen last night had *Venifucus* tattoos. You saw them. They were here for either you or the kid. Maybe both. They might've toyed with you for a while, but you can be sure you'd die in the end. That's what they do. They are sworn to kill all the Others on the side of Light and bring back their evil leader, Elspeth, Destroyer of Worlds."

Jesse was punching keys on the laptop as he spoke, accessing the internet and one of his accounts where his brother could reach him. They'd used this same system to keep in touch many times while Jesse had been halfway around the world, fighting in some godforsaken hellhole. He'd always been able to count on little bro to keep in touch and ground him to his roots, his home. Jason was all about the Pack. He was a good Alpha who cared for his people and his family.

"I guess someone doesn't get to be called the Destroyer of Worlds for no reason at all, huh?" Maria seemed both deflated and yet resolved.

"You've got that right, I'm sorry to say." A window opened on the laptop and there was Jason, his baby brother. Jesse used the mic pickup on the laptop to test the connection. "Can you hear me, Jay?"

"Loud and clear, Jess." His voice came through a little tinny on the built-in speakers. It wasn't great, but it would do. "The Lords are rounding up someone who might be able to convince your bear shifter. One of their people thinks he knows the juvenile you're dealing with."

"Excellent. Do you have an ETA?"

"About ten minutes, they said."

"Good."

"In the meantime, Sally was wondering if Dr. Garibaldi was available."

"Hang on a sec. I'll check." Jesse muted the sound and moved away from the camera. He didn't want to put Maria on the spot. If she wasn't ready to see and talk to her cousin, he wasn't about to force her. "Sally wants to speak to you, but you don't have to if you're not ready yet. We'll see her soon enough when we get to Wyoming."

"No, it's okay. I'd like to see what she looks like. Even if I'm not totally convinced we're actually related." Maria came over to sit in front of the coffee table where he'd set up the laptop.

Jesse set it to receive audio again and leaned into camera range beside Maria.

"Jason, this is Maria. Maria, my brother, Jason." Jesse figured he'd keep it to first names to make things easier. Maria probably didn't know much about the shifter world or how to properly address an Alpha. Better to treat her as they did regular humans, by the customs of the human world. He'd set them all on equal footing.

Maria was taken aback by how different the brothers were. Sure, they had very similar features, and the man on the screen looked somewhat younger than the guy in her living room, but it wasn't so much the years as the mileage. Jesse's eyes were...haunted was the best word she could find. He'd seen things that had left their mark on his soul.

Sensitive as she was to wounded things, she felt it and saw it every time she looked at him. Yet there was a core of strength in Jesse that refused to give up or give in.

"Pleased to meet you," Maria said gently, trying to keep her thoughts from spilling over into her tone.

"Same here. My wife has been looking forward to talking with you. I'll give her the chair." Maria watched as the man stood, his jeans-clad crotch filling the screen for a moment.

She almost laughed but figured Jesse wouldn't appreciate her humor. A second later, Jason was gone and a dark-haired woman was taking his place in the chair in front of their computer. She put on the headset Jason, now off-camera, handed her. And then she smiled.

Maria couldn't help but answer that smile with one of her own. The woman's face was more angular than her own, but Maria saw something in her eyes, the curve of her brows...something familiar.

"So you're supposed to be my cousin?" Maria found herself speaking her thoughts aloud.

"I am. My name is Sally, and I've been asked to find you by our mutual ancestor, a woman named Leonora. She's a dryad."

"So I've heard," Maria said dryly, shooting Jesse a glance. He seemed very interested in her first conversation with this other woman. "I just don't really understand how it could be. My family is only a little magical. Some of my father's relatives believe in magic, but my dad died when I was a child. So far, my only gift has been with wild animals."

"Wait a minute," Jesse said, drawing her attention. "Some of your relatives are magic users? What gift do you have?" His gaze condemned her for not coming clean sooner, and she bristled.

"My nona and aunt are both witches, I guess you'd call them. They do spells, dance under the full moon and things like that. My mother always thought they were crazy, but when I was little, I realized that occasionally I could feel the energy of the forest and its creatures. My nona said I had healing talent and helped set me on the path toward veterinary school. She felt so strongly about it, she even paid for my education. Mom and my stepfather wanted nothing to do with it. They wanted me to be a lawyer. My stepfather's a very successful attorney. Mom's a society wife with a drinking problem, if I'm being brutally honest. I think she started drinking when my father died. I always felt she married Frank on the rebound, trying to forget my real father."

"I'm sorry," came Sally's understanding voice over the small speakers. "I never knew my parents. I was raised by foster families and never really thought I had any family out there until I met Leonora a few weeks ago. She showed me that the affinity I always had for growing things came from her influence in my ancestry. It seems we part-dryads are able to make our family tree visible by using our magic to call it. That's how I know you are one of my cousins and that I have a sister I've never met. My line descends from Leonora's daughter, Marisol, who married a werewolf several centuries ago, so I have a bit of werewolf in me. Not enough to shift or anything, sorry to say. In me, the dryad magic is much stronger than anything else. I can make plants grow and hear the song of the forest. Trees speak to me."

Maria shifted on her seat, uncomfortable with the description. Part of what she heard was very familiar to her and something she'd denied for a long time because of her mother's disapproval. Maria had consciously limited herself to healing animals. Talking to trees had been strictly forbidden by her class-conscious mother from the time she was old enough to toddle.

"I'm a vet. I heal animals, and usually only in the conventional way. Occasionally, I think magic comes into it."

"You deal mostly with forest creatures, right? Wolves, mountain lions, bears? Jason said you run a sanctuary for wild animals," Sally prompted.

Maria found herself nodding. "Those are the creatures I'm drawn to help the most."

"Makes sense." Sally shrugged. "They are part of the woodland too. They are part of what we were born to protect and nurture."

"I still don't know if I believe all of this. I mean, I know about shifters. I've dealt with one once before, and just a few minutes ago I saw a bear turn into a teenager in my guest room. I know they're real. And I know magic is real. But I don't know if I believe I'm part-dryad, or that I'm related to you. I think Nona or my aunt would've known if we had other relatives out there. They're all about family. Especially Nona. She keeps track of everyone and holds the family together."

"I'd love to meet them." Sally's voice was filled with an eager sort of longing and a tiny bit of pain. Maria remembered then that this woman—a strong, capable police woman from all accounts—had never really had a family of her own. Maria's heart went out to her.

"I'm sure they'd love to meet you too, Sally. Once this crisis is over, why don't we all get together and figure out where you come from and how my family fits in?"

A smile broke over the woman's face on the screen. "I'd love that. Thank you."

"You're welcome. Frankly, I'm really intrigued by all of this and willing to listen—more now than when your brother-in-law broke down my kitchen door in the middle of the night." She chuckled, shooting a mock glare at Jesse.

"Speaking of which, Maria, you need to be really careful. The guys who tried to snatch you don't mess around. Those men were part of a group that shot a teenage girl from the Pack, trying to abduct her. Failing that, they grabbed a young boy and set up a highly explosive booby trap for anyone who tried to rescue him. These are not nice people. Terrorists with a magical agenda."

"They want their Destroyer of Worlds back, right? Jesse was just telling me about it."

"Jason and Jesse know more about that than I do. I'm pretty new to all this. I only found out about Others a month ago. Before that, I lived in San Francisco and didn't really understand much about the magical world. Only that I could make things grow. But living in the city, I was limited to urban gardens and potted plants."

"I can't imagine living in the city. I grew up on an estate with a big manicured garden and lots of animals. My stepfather had an apartment in the city where he'd stay over if he was on a case. Otherwise, he'd commute a few days a week."

"My, my. I'm not sure we're socially acceptable among the country-club crowd," Jesse joked, listening in. She made a face at him and Sally laughed on the other end of the connection, having heard Jesse's words through the laptop speaker.

"In case you haven't noticed, I gave all that up to live out here with the animals. I call this place a sanctuary for a reason." Maria rolled her eyes at Jesse and then sobered. "I thought I was safe way out here in the middle of nowhere, but this morning proved me wrong in a big way."

Sally looked grim when Maria refocused on the screen. "The hunters shot Leonora with a silver bullet. You know silver is poison to magical folk, right? The forest is keeping her alive for now, but she's the main reason I'm so eager to find all of my relations quickly. She said we need to put our energies together to heal her. The sooner we can do that, the better."

Maria could tell Sally felt very strongly about the dryad. Maria's tender heart was touched by the unspoken plea in

Sally's voice. Maria would think long and hard about this as she got to know these people better. She was wary by nature, but if her instincts were correct and they were on the level, she would do all she could to help Sally and Leonora.

She just had to get through the current crisis first.

At that moment, Jason's hand appeared on Sally's shoulder on the screen. The other woman looked up for a moment and then turned back to the screen.

"Jason says the Lords are ready to talk to your guest. I'll sign off for now, but I hope we can talk again soon."

"I'd like that. Nice talking to you, Sally."

"You too, Maria. Bye." Maria watched Sally remove the headset and hand it back to Jason. Maria was treated to another crotch shot as they changed places in front of the camera and had to hold back a giggle.

"It's show time," Jesse said, reaching for the laptop. He'd already unplugged it. It would run on battery power for an hour or so. Probably much longer than they'd need.

Maria followed Jesse into the hall and paused when he did to knock on the doorframe of the guest room. Zach was still in bed with his eyes closed, but he opened them the moment Jesse knocked. He was alert but also clearly still exhausted and in a bit of pain.

"I've got my brother and the Lords on video chat. They want to talk to you, Zach." Jesse walked into the room and left the laptop on the nightstand while he helped the teen sit up. He then transferred the laptop to the kid's lap. "Just talk, they'll hear you through the laptop's mic."

Maria stayed by the door, not wanting to upset Zach.

"Hi," the kid said, his voice filled with doubt and uncertainty.

"I'm Jason Moore, Alpha of the Wyoming wolf Pack." Jason's voice rang with an authority he hadn't used when talking to Maria.

"I mean no disrespect, Alpha, but I don't know you, and people who said they were friends have turned out to be enemies lately."

Maria heard Jason's audible sigh. "I understand, son. Which is why I called the Lords on your behalf. I'm going to patch through the video now. Hopefully they can convince you."

There was a moment's pause and then Maria saw the teen's shoulders stiffen. She couldn't see the screen but assumed the so-called Lords had replaced the image of Jason Moore.

"Zach, is it?" a new voice asked through the computer's speakers. "I'm Tim and this is my brother, Rafe. We have someone here who thinks he knows you."

There was another pause and then Maria clearly saw tears form in the teen's eyes.

"Uncle Rocky?" The youngster's voice was filled with emotion. Hope, fear, joy, sorrow, and most of all, relief.

"Zach, my boy, what happened to you?" A gruff, deeper voice came through the speakers, filled with urgency and tinged with anger at what had been done to the kid on the other side of the connection. "Where are your parents?"

"Captured trying to give me a chance to escape." The kid broke down at that point, tears falling from his eyes, but his determination helped him remain strong and able to talk through his heartache. "I ran, but I'd already been slashed by silver. I was weak and my magic was blocked by the poison and something I've never felt before. Really evil, sinister magic. And then they shot me. I managed to keep running as long as I could, but I ended up in somebody's backyard and humans caught me. I thought that was better at the time. They drugged me and I woke up in a cage."

Colorful cursing came from the other end of the computer connection.

"The doctor smelled like magic, but she treated me like an animal. She says she didn't know I was a shifter, but I'm not sure. And then the wolf showed up and he took me out of the cage and brought me into her house, where I am now." The rambling words made the young man sound more like the frightened teen he really was.

"I've been briefed about where you are, Zach. The doc runs a sanctuary for wild animals. From all reports, she really doesn't know much about us, though she hosted a female of the Cougar Clan once. She probably didn't realize you were a shifter. I'd give her the benefit of the doubt, because the moment Jesse told her what you were, they got you out of the cage, right?"

"Yes, Uncle Rocky." The kid sounded both contrite and obedient. He must really respect his uncle.

"Now about the wolf. I know his brother, Jason, the Alpha, and I know him too, son. He's a good man. One who will protect you with his life. I know this from personal experience. I've fought at his side and know him for an honorable man. He's on our side in this, Zach. You can trust him."

Maria was surprised to hear that kind of personal endorsement, but she wasn't surprised that Jesse was well-respected by his peers. He'd proven, just in these few short hours, to be a capable leader and man of honor.

She was going to leave with him on some kind of odyssey to discover her real place in the magical world. Well, that and to avoid being attacked in her own home again by the same bastards that had shot the young bear and captured his parents. The thought of his parents suffering somewhere at the hands of such cruel people made her blood boil.

If she was going to leave her sanctuary, she needed to make arrangements. Maria left the hallway and headed into her office. She had to make a series of phone calls to be certain her animal guests would be well taken care of in her absence.

Chapter Four

"She's gone," Jesse observed when the conversation over the computer paused. "We can speak freely." He'd tilted the laptop so both he and Zach were in the frame while they consulted with the Lords and the weregrizzly, Rocky, about how best to proceed. He'd known Maria was in the hall, but hadn't objected. Still, there were some things he'd rather not have her hear.

They'd been questioning Zach about what he remembered from before he was shot. It seemed the kidnappers were in Nebraska. Zach and his family had lived in Aurora, just west of Lincoln. He remembered being driven around for about an hour and then being held at a farm. There had been a big house and a stable full of very high-strung horses whose whinnies of fear hurt his ears.

"As soon as we end this call, I'm on my way to Nebraska, but it's going to take time for me to get there. You're the closest, most capable operative we have in the area, Jesse. I know you'll have the doc in tow, but she could be helpful too, if anyone's been hurt. And she's got magic. Maybe it's untrained, but you said she saw the *Venifucus* tattoos, so she's got some power and an ability you don't. She could help you spot them, if nothing else. Somehow, I think she could be of use on this mission," Rocky tried to convince him.

"I don't want to put her in even more danger, Rock. I came here to protect her, not make her part of an assault team with very little chance of success."

"At least do the recon. When I get there, I'm going in guns blazing. It would help if I knew what I was walking into,"

Rocky's voice was firm, demanding.

Jesse thought about it for a moment. He had Zach—their only eye witness to what had happened to his parents. And Zach had already volunteered to go back and show Jesse where everything had gone down. He could at least follow the trail as long as it was safe, but he didn't know eastern Nebraska at all. For that, the doc would come in handy. She'd grown up around here and lived on her sanctuary outside Davenport for the past few years, but the original address Sally had found for her had been on the outskirts of Lincoln, Nebraska, where her parents still lived. She would probably know the route from there to here and back again reasonably well.

"All right. It's on our way back to Wyoming." He sighed, not liking where this was going but seeing no other way. "I'll scout for you. But you'd better bust your ass getting there, Rock. I don't like putting either one of them in more danger."

"Hold on." Rocky rustled some papers on the other end of the connection. "Weather's going to play a role here. All flights are grounded on my end, so I'll have to go by ground transport. That's going to add time to my ETA. Also, the weather is heading in your direction. Severe thunderstorm warnings and tornado watches are going up all over the place. You'd better keep one eye to the sky, Jess."

He had noticed it getting cloudier, and his sinuses had told him the barometer had definitely dropped, but he hadn't realized the severity of what they were forecasting. "I won't expect you tomorrow then."

"If the weather plays nice. Dammit!" Rocky growled over the speakers. "Of all the times for severe storms, this takes the cake. I'm sorry, Zach. I'll get to you as quick as I can. We'll get your parents out of danger and tear apart the bastards who shot you. I promise."

"I know, Uncle Rocky. Thanks," Zach said in a remarkably steady voice. He was gaining strength even as Jesse watched him. He'd relaxed his wary stance. Seeing his uncle had done that for him. Allowed him to relax so his magic could flow and heal him. Thank the Lady for modern technology that allowed the kid to see his uncle's face over the video chat.

"Rocky, there's one other thing you should know." Jesse had realized something as soon as the kid had identified Rocky as his uncle.

"Yeah?"

"The doctor's last name is Garibaldi."

"You don't say." Rocky's voice turned pensive.

"Quite a coincidence, isn't it?"

"Who are her people?" Rocky was quick to ask.

"You can get what few details we have from my brother's new mate. I know her stepdad and mom live outside of Lincoln. She's related through her father's bloodline to the dryad Leonora who lives in our woods, and she described both her grandmother and aunt as witches."

"So she descends from magical folk." Rocky trailed off, thinking, but came back a moment later. "Well, it's something to investigate. For now, we need to protect Zach and the woman, and help my sister and her mate, if they can still be helped. I think I'd know if she was dead. She's not. Right, Zach?"

"Definitely," Zach agreed. "They're still alive. I can feel it."

"Good. Hold on to that. And if you can, use your connection to them to help Jesse figure out where they are. I'm coming and I'm bringing reinforcements. We'll get your folks and bring them to safety. I swear."

"Thanks, Uncle Rocky." The kid choked up, unable to say more, and Jesse patted his shoulder.

He turned the laptop and started making plans with the Lords. Rocky had left, already gathering supplies and a bit of help before hitting the road. He'd stay in touch by phone and the Lords would coordinate anything that needed coordination on a larger scale. They gave Jesse Rocky's direct cell number and he punched it into his phone, sending Rocky a text that had all his contact information. They'd be able to communicate directly now—as long as they were both in range of a cell tower and the storms didn't interfere too much.

Jesse spent a few more minutes talking with the Lords before they signed off and Jason was back on his screen. They discussed manpower and which of Jesse's select group of ex-Special Forces soldiers they could send to help. In less than five minutes, they'd ended the video chat and Jesse powered down the laptop.

"We're going to have to move fast, Zach. Are you up to it?"

Zach nodded, still overcome by the emotion that seeing his uncle and knowing he was in the presence of friends rather than enemies had inspired. Jesse understood. The kid had been through a lot in the past days.

"All right. Rest here for now. I'm going to scrounge some clothes for you and help the doc pack up. We'll be hitting the road shortly, but I want you to rest as much as possible before we do. Got it?" He smiled to soften his orders and the kid responded with a shaky smile of his own as Jesse headed out the door.

They'd lucked out in a way. Rocky had been able to convince Zach he was among friends much more easily than anyone else could have. And now it was just possible that the doc and Rocky—and Zach too—were somehow related. Both the doc and Rocky's last name was Garibaldi. Something to ponder later, as Rocky had said, but something that reassured Jesse that the Lady was working in Her mysterious ways to bring all these different players together.

Jesse found Maria in her office, just hanging up the phone as she scrambled to collect some papers and a checkbook, which she threw into her oversized pocketbook. The bag was bulging, so she must've been collecting things from the office since she left him and Zach to talk on the computer.

"Do you have a case for this?" Jesse asked, lifting the laptop he still held in one hand.

"In the corner over there." She gestured with her chin since her hands were still full.

Jesse searched and found a backpack-style computer case made of padded nylon that would be both very protective and easy to carry. The computer slid into one compartment and there were other sections that would hold the charger, wireless modem, mouse and various cables that might be needed to connect to a printer, projector or high-speed internet connection. She had almost all contingencies covered and still had room in the backpack for other stuff.

"You'll need to pack some clothes and Zach needs something to wear. I have a spare set of fatigues in my bag—"

"You have a bag?" she cut him off, turning her surprised gaze on him.

"Stashed in an old oak on the edge of your property." He shrugged. "Problem is, Zach isn't quite full grown yet. He'd fit better in a pair of your sweats, I think. If you have any. He'd look a lot less conspicuous if he's seen."

She rolled her eyes but bit back whatever it was she'd been about to say when her phone rang. She placed her hand on the receiver and answered him. "I'll find something for him." Then she picked up the phone and answered. "Sanctuary." She placed the phone between her ear and her shoulder as she continued to rummage around the office. He'd been dismissed.

Jesse had to smile as he walked out to the living room, collecting the laptop charger and stowing it in the backpack. He raided her cabinets looking for snack food that would keep without refrigeration and threw some of that into the front of the backpack, along with a few items that could be used as survival tools—waterproof matches, a Swiss Army knife and some other things he found—until the bag was full. The rest of the snacks, he put in a plastic shopping bag.

Then he went to the fridge and made a bunch of sandwiches, putting them in the cooler he'd found stashed in one of the closets. Cold sodas followed, along with whatever else looked good and easy to eat while on the move. A picnic bag of plastic utensils and bottled water went in as well as paper cups and a bottle of juice.

Zach was a growing boy. He'd be hungry as he healed. Jesse gobbled two giant sandwiches as he worked, not having eaten in quite a while. He needed fuel too. He put aside a smaller sandwich for Maria. She needed to eat too, and he'd be sure she had at least a sandwich before they took off.

"My friends are coming over to take care of the animals. Do you want to do a quick run through to make sure I don't have any other shifters caged?" She made a face and he could see again how bad she felt about Zach.

"We'll do that on the way out. I don't want to leave you or Zach on your own in case they send in the A Team this time. The guys last night were definitely the B Team. We'd already dealt with their friends back in Wyoming. The *Venifucus* definitely didn't send their elite forces when they sent those guys." Jesse handed her the sandwich he'd made for her after she placed her bag on the kitchen table next to the laptop backpack and the cooler he'd stocked.

"Okay, but my car is in the front. We'll have to double back."

"We won't be taking your car. It's too slow and too easy to trace. I have a rented four-by-four waiting in the woods. We can check your guests as we make our way to the SUV." She looked like she wanted to argue, but he pushed the sandwich at her. "Eat. You'll need the fuel."

She cracked a smile and picked up the sandwich. It looked huge in her delicate hands. "Now you sound like my nona. She's always telling me I'm too skinny. She refuses to believe I really need to lose about thirty pounds."

Jesse paused and let his gaze run over her. He knew his tongue was practically hanging out of his mouth, but he couldn't help himself.

"As far as I'm concerned, you're perfect, Doc." He heard the growl escape his throat and walked his gaze up her luscious body to meet her gaze. She seemed not only shocked but...aroused?

He sniffed the air as he stepped closer to her. Oh, yeah. She was definitely aroused. Fuck. She smelled so damn good.

He was instantly hard and ready to go. He wanted her bad. His wolf wanted to sink his teeth—and his cock—into her and fuck her senseless. He wanted to hear her scream his name as she came around him, taking him with her to the moon.

He put his arms around her and tugged her close to his body. He had enough presence of mind to take the sandwich out of her hands and place it back on the table behind her. Then the beast was in control. It pulled her against him with a single hard tug that startled her. She gasped when her soft body met his hardness. Her eyes widened as she gazed up into his eyes. Caught. He was hers.

Jesse's head dipped and he captured her lips with his. The kiss started savage and then...morphed. It changed into something much more serious than the blind lust that had ridden him to this point.

He hadn't meant to touch her, but he hadn't been able to help himself. The scent of her arousal was more than he could take. He had to taste her, sample her sweetness, claim it for himself, even if just for this moment out of time.

She tangled her hands in the short hair at the base of his neck. Her body strained against him as she responded. She wasn't just a recipient of his kiss, she was a full participant in the lust that ignited from the kiss into a conflagration neither of them could deny or control.

Jesse backed her against the table, lifting her until she sat on the very edge. He nudged her legs apart with his hips, taking his place between them as their mouths continued to consume each other, driving the fire that had flared between them higher.

Jesse dragged his lips from hers and began nibbling his way down her throat, pausing in the delicately scented place in the crook of her neck, nosing under her soft brown hair. She smelled so damn good. Like ambrosia. Like the finest wine. Delicious.

He kept moving lower, shaping her ribs one by one with his fingers, then moving higher, supporting her generous breasts. She was built like a woman with a capital W. Just the way he liked his women. Not scrawny or overly muscular, but luscious and stacked with generous hips and an ass he could sink his teeth into. Hot damn.

She wasn't stopping him as his nose found its way down into the V of her blouse and he worked his hands up over her bra to cup her and mold her. Satisfaction growled through him when her nipples bloomed against the palms of his hands. He pinched gently and learning her shape.

And a fine shape it was, indeed. He couldn't wait. The beast wanted to taste her skin. He pulled on the cotton of her shirt, ripping it with a single tug. Buttons bounced off his chest, the small projectiles making little zaps against his T-shirt. He didn't feel it. The only thing that really registered was the white lace of her bra. Her hard nipples poked outward, their darker color clear against the translucent lace. He wanted to howl in approval.

Down, boy.

Her hands still tangled in his hair, silent encouragement for him to go farther. He wasn't about to argue. He pulled down the lace cups until her luscious tits popped free with a happy bounce. He almost grinned, but the desire to lick her won out.

Jesse leaned closer and ran his tongue up the crease between her breasts, then over to the right in a spiraling motion, closer and closer, over her soft skin to the pointy center that seemed to strain for his attention. The taste of her skin was absolutely addictive. He sucked her nipple into his mouth and teased it with his tongue. He liked the way she shivered in his arms. She was so responsive that he knew she loved what he was doing to her.

Sucking and moving his head back, he let that nipple go with a little wet pop, admiring the way it stood out from the incredibly soft and supple mound of her generous breast. Her skin was pale, as if the sun never touched it, and the pointed tip had grown even pinker than it had been due to his attentions. He liked the way it looked and he decided he wanted to see a matched set.

Without preamble this time, he dove for and found the other nipple, pointed and waiting for him. He was a little bit rougher with this one, seeing how far he could push her. She took it all, writhing against him as she slid her hands under his shirt and around his back, pulling him closer. The way she touched him nearly drove him out of his mind.

He nipped gently on her bud, growling low in his throat when she scratched a path lightly over his back and around to his abdomen. She didn't mark him, but he felt the blunt tips of her short nails with every fiber of his being. Seemed like it was his turn to shiver with pleasure.

Jesse slipped one hand beneath the waistband of her pants and lacy panties. There was just enough room for him to cup her pussy and insert one finger between her slippery folds. She creamed when he rubbed her clit, bathing his hand in her essence. He wanted to taste it, but something else was driving him beyond his own pleasure.

He wanted to see her come. Desperately.

He'd known this woman just a few hours and he couldn't go on another minute without knowing what she looked like when she came for him. It was a basic need. An almost animalistic desire. The wolf inside him wanted to paw and claim, slam her down on all fours and fuck her from behind, mastering her. The man wanted to see her eyes dilate with passion, wanted to hold her gaze as she came at his command. Only then would he be satisfied.

Well...he wouldn't be completely satisfied until he got his dick inside her and bathed her womb with his seed. But he didn't have time for that now. Even as he lost control to pleasure, the small, working part of his mind knew they had to leave. Every moment they delayed was a moment of possible danger to this woman and the boy.

Every protective instinct inside him wanted to keep her safe. Keep her in his arms. Keep her. Period.

Whoa. That sounded serious, but he couldn't really concentrate enough at the moment to care. He moved his finger farther up her slit, seeking entrance.

He released her nipple from his mouth with a last long, lingering lick, then met her gaze as he pushed his finger inside her tight channel. Oh, yeah. Her body began to flutter in excitement, her cunt squeezing his finger the way he wanted it to squeeze his cock. Damn. She was tight in a way that told him she hadn't had sex in a very long time.

His mouth began to water at the idea of sticking his dick in the molten heat that milked his finger as her body began moving almost involuntarily. She wanted more. She was begging for it.

The pants limited his ability to move his hand, but she was trying to ride him anyway.

And then her fingers found his nipples under his T-shirt. It was like an electric shock went through him at her touch.

"Fuck this," he muttered, using his free hand to unbutton and unzip her pants.

She lifted up eagerly for him to push them down over her shapely ass. They bunched up around her knees, but she was able to spread her legs a little wider and his hand was free to move as he began to stroke in and out of her tight pussy.

He wanted to growl. He wanted to bite. He wanted to fuck her with more than just his hand. A small growl rumbled through his chest and she flattened her palms over his pecs, seeming to soak in the sound that made his chest vibrate. Her gaze held his in silent plea.

"I want you so bad it hurts, Maria. Will you let me have you?" She'd never know how much it cost him to ask and not to simply claim her as the wolf inside him wanted so badly to do.

"I ache for you."

Her simple answer was all he needed. That and the way she moved on his hand, fucking his finger, her body almost out of control, needing so much more than that. He read the need in her gaze. She wasn't holding back. She wanted him. She wanted him bad. Almost as much as he wanted her.

He removed his finger from her wet pussy, pleased when she whimpered at the loss.

"Hold on, babe," he whispered, staying close to her while removing her pants completely.

She kicked off her shoes to help, her eager movements spurring him on. Her little hands tugged his T-shirt up to his armpits and he got the idea she wanted it gone. No problem. A quick yank over his head and it was lost on the floor behind him.

Her hands went immediately to his shoulders, pulling him closer. He looked into her eyes, seeing what he'd hoped to see. Her green irises were dilated with need. Need for him. Oh, yeah, that's what he'd been longing to see.

Jesse wasted little time unbuttoning his fly and pushing his pants down far enough to free his aching cock. He stepped closer, pulling her bare ass to the edge of the table, at a good enough height to make this workable. He'd bend over her and shove home, using the table for balance. He could see it all in his mind.

But Maria had other ideas. She reached for his cock, those clever hands of hers learning his length and width, rubbing and stroking in ways that nearly blew his head off. She tried to bend and take him in her mouth, but he wouldn't allow it. The first time he wanted to be inside her when he came. He was just caveman enough to need to claim her the old fashioned way. Cock in pussy, man on top.

And it was the man in control in this situation. If the wolf had more of a hold over him, he'd be bending her over and claiming her from behind. Doggy style. Oh, he wanted to do that to her eventually, but not at the moment. With this magical human woman, he had to be more man than beast, even if he was a little rougher around the edges than any man she'd ever had before.

He'd make her forget anyone she'd ever had. He'd be all she needed. Ever.

Again, the possessive thoughts that should have set off alarm bells just skittered through his brain. He wasn't alarmed. He was horny as hell and in need of a hard fuck. A hard fuck with this woman and only this woman. No other would do at the moment. Probably no other woman would do for him again. Ever.

So be it. If this was the mate the goddess had chosen for him, who was he to argue?

He stepped closer to her, lowering enough to make things easier.

"Put it in, babe. Line it up and accept me." He sent a silent prayer to the Lady that Maria wouldn't wake up and refuse him now. It was suddenly important to him that she make this final step and actively participate in the claiming.

That wasn't how it was usually done among wolves, but Maria wasn't a wolf. She was something altogether more alluring. Something new in his experience. Something he wanted with all his heart. The wolf pushed him to take her, but his human half knew she had to do more than meekly accept. She had to choose.

She met his gaze, her eyes searching his while her fingers moved him into position.

"Come into me now, Jesse. I want you so much." Her words were the barest whisper, but he heard them and took them into his heart, into his mind as he pushed forward, her dainty fingers guiding him as he took his time, going slow because he knew she was so tight.

It was heaven and it was hell, all wrapped up into one. The hell was having to go so slow for fear of hurting her. The heaven was the way her tight body wrapped around him like a fist, squeezing and milking, coaxing him deeper as it gave up its slippery welcome to ease his way.

Finally, he was in deep. As far as he could go. Home.

It was perfection. Their eyes held throughout, and her gaze glazed over again as he began to move the barest fraction of an inch.

He loved the way her body welcomed him, blossoming under his assault, giving more and more of herself. Jesse began to move in earnest, knowing this first climax would be hard and fast. Judging by her response to him, she wouldn't mind. They were in synch. He could even feel their hearts beginning to beat in time with each other. Something he'd never felt before with any woman he'd fucked, be they wolf bitch or human.

He'd never had a mage though. At least not that he knew of. Maybe Maria's as yet undetermined brand of magic had some effect. This had already been the most significant conquest he'd ever made from the way he'd needed to be where he was now to the way he'd wanted her to take an active part in the claiming. He'd never felt anything like this before and certainly not the level of extreme passion that was beginning to make any sort of coherent thought impossible.

He let instinct take over since it had guided him so well to this moment. He lay her down on the table, spread out before him as he bent over her, using his hands on either side of her head to support his weight. She wrapped her legs around his waist, her little heels digging into his ass in the most delicious way as she spurred him on.

She almost tried to direct his fucking. No woman had ever tried to control him before. He wasn't altogether sure he liked the connotation of her wanting more control, but his body certainly enjoyed her efforts and enthusiasm. From the direction of her heels digging into his ass, he could tell she wanted it faster and harder. Just what the doctor ordered, because that's what he wanted more than anything in the world at the moment.

Jesse set to work, fucking like a bucking bronco, pounding into her just the way they both wanted. He watched her face as he claimed her squirming body over and over, dominating her while she held all the real power. If she said no at any point, he'd have to leave, even if it killed him. Her wishes were that important to him.

But she wasn't saying no. In fact, she was panting, whispering, "Yes, yes, yes." In time with his thrusts. As he moved faster, feeling the crisis drawing close for both of them, he added a little motion with his hips on the end of each thrust. It was just enough to send her over the edge.

She keened lightly as she came, and he watched her beautiful face as rapture took her. He'd never forget the sight, even as his own passion drove him onward.

She hadn't quite come down from that first peak when another hit her even harder. He pushed through it, watching her reactions and gauging her desires. Then another peak hit that looked and felt even higher as her channel milked his hard cock. He was nearing his limit when she cried out for a final time and dug her nails into his shoulders, almost deep enough to draw blood.

He didn't mind. It was as if he were waiting for that final

signal to ram into her and let every muscle in his body go tense as his balls emptied in a hot rush of come that coated her insides and made his passage even easier. The exquisite rigor lasted long moments while she held his gaze and both of them quaked with the most amazing pleasure he'd ever experienced.

His breathing was as erratic as hers when the almost miraculous rapture began to ease. Silence reigned as their breath slowly began to return and their hearts—now most definitely beating in time—began to slow.

"I hope you don't think I do this all the time." She was still breathless, which made him want to smile for no apparent reason except that he'd managed to tire her out with a series of mind-blowing orgasms.

"I know you don't." He grinned and lowered his head to kiss her with just a hint of the hunger he still had for her, though it had mostly abated for the moment after that grand climax.

Her eyebrows drew together in confusion. "How do you know?"

"You were tighter than a nun's wimple, sweetheart. I know I'm the first man to fuck you in a long time." And didn't that make him so proud he could bust his buttons if he had any that weren't currently unbuttoned.

"A nun's what?" She looked so adorably confused that he had to kiss her again. When he let her up for air a long time later, they'd both more or less forgotten the question.

Her legs released their grip on his waist as her body relaxed and he drew away, knowing she had to be a little uncomfortable with the hard kitchen table against her back. Her shirt was in ruins, her bra still pushing her tits up and together, a sight that made his mouth water, even after he'd gotten his rocks off.

"Damn, you're beautiful."

She smiled and her cheeks blushed the prettiest pink he'd seen outside her magnificent nipples. He scooped his arms under her back and helped support her as she sat up. They were still joined. He was oddly loath to pull out of her warm, welcoming body.

"I'm glad you think so." She seemed shy now, after the fact, even with his cock still inside her.

"I don't want to leave," he admitted as their gazes locked and held.

She giggled and the sound enchanted him. "It'd be a little hard to get anything done if we went around joined at the hip, so to speak."

He had to join her amusement. "Yeah, but think about the compensations. We could fuck all the time and the pleasure..." He couldn't even put it into words.

"Yeah," she agreed softly. "I've never felt anything like it." The admission touched him deeply. He leaned forward and rested his forehead against hers.

"I still don't want to leave, but I know I have to. The longer we stay here, the more likely we'll get caught with our pants down."

"Or off," she added with a mischievous smile.

He winked at her. "The next time we make love, I want you completely naked. And I want to spend all night—or day—or however long we have, learning your every curve, your every shiver, your every desire."

Damn, he was getting hot again just thinking about it.

"I want that too," she admitted softly. "But right now, I think I'd better grab a quick shower before we go."

He knew she was right, but he didn't have to like it. He disengaged from her body slowly, knowing she had to be tender and not wanting to cause her any discomfort. He hated being apart from her already.

"Okay. I'll be good. Go grab a shower, but make it quick. We really have to get on the road as soon as possible." He bent down and placed a lingering kiss on her lips. He loved her taste and he was already addicted to it.

He moved away, allowing her room to stand while she straightened the cups of her bra and tried to pull her buttonless shirt back together somehow. He bent and retrieved her pants from the floor. She still wore her socks, but he found the lacy scrap of her panties mixed up inside her pants. He handed the pants back, but kept the panties.

He made sure she saw when he pulled up his fatigue pants and tucked the lacy white panties into his pocket. This way, he'd have her scent with him at all times. Something he wanted. Something he was beginning to need. He didn't understand it all completely yet, but something momentous had just occurred.

He thought maybe he'd just fucked his mate for the very first time. The panties would be his trophy for now. Eventually, he would have her promise and a ring on her finger in the traditions of her world, claiming her for all to see, marrying their lives together for all time.

Just maybe.

If they lived through the next few days.

Chapter Five

Maria fled the kitchen with her pants clutched to her chest as she flew up the stairs to her bedroom and the attached master bath. What had just happened? How had she ended up naked from the waist down, having sex on the kitchen table with a man she'd just met?

What kind of weird sexual pull did the wolf man have on her? And most importantly, why did she want to do it all again? And again. And again. Oh, Lord, she had it bad.

Maria stopped in her bedroom and stripped, throwing her clothes in the hamper and grabbing a shorts set that was one of her favorites. It was comfy and nice looking. She wanted to look as good as possible, knowing she'd be traveling with Jesse for a while. Feminine vanity reared its ugly head—something she hadn't been prone to in too many years to count. Darn it. The furry fool downstairs had her primping and preening.

Of course, he'd given her the best orgasm she'd ever experienced. Make that *multiple* orgasms. She'd never done *that* before. Just remembering the way he'd coaxed her body to respond made her rub her thighs together and squirm. Mmm. He was really *that* good.

Maria took a shower. Luckily she'd always been quick getting ready in the morning. Ten minutes and she was dried and dressed and ready to go. She paused in her bedroom, looking for clothes she wanted to bring with her. She had a small duffel bag with a long strap that was easy to carry over her shoulder. She used it when she visited her family and stayed overnight.

She found a few pairs of roomy sweats that looked like they

would fit Zach. He was a teenager, growing fast, but he was only a few inches taller than her. His shoulders were already a lot wider. He would be a big man when he finished growing, but for now he'd be able to fit into the stretchy, soft cotton fleece she had in abundance.

Maria wore a lot of sweatshirts, hoodies and sweatpants in the winter when she had to go outside in the snow to see to her animal guests. Her line of work meant she got dirty often and sometimes had to go through several changes of clothes a day. Her closet held more than enough for both herself and the teen.

She'd be able to give him a brand new bag of tube socks too. She'd bought men's athletic socks by mistake the last time she'd been to the big superstore down by the interstate and hadn't had a chance to bring them back yet. Something told her perhaps the mistake she'd made on that last shopping trip hadn't been such a mistake after all. Her nona always said the Lady worked in mysterious ways.

A shiver raced up her spine. Perhaps somewhere deep down where her grandmother swore Maria's fledgling magic lived, she'd known to prepare for what was coming. She'd had flashes of clairvoyance before. Nothing explicit really, but she always knew when the animals were getting into trouble and when to go out into the pens and help them. Nona called it her sixth sense, but it had never driven her to unintentionally buy men's socks before.

Well, stranger things had happened in her life. Including having sex with someone she'd just met on her kitchen table. A wave of heat flushed her cheeks as she remembered the way he'd mastered her body so easily. Damn, that man was good. She was getting all hot and bothered just remembering how he'd pushed her body to the edge of ecstasy and beyond. So far beyond. To a place she'd never been before.

Oh yeah. The man knew how to please a woman. More importantly, Jesse knew how to please *her*. Like no other she'd ever had before. Not that there'd been many. He'd been right about that. Maria hadn't had sex in a couple of years. And before that, there hadn't exactly been a queue waiting for her attention.

No, Maria was usually much more selective about who she invited into her bed. Too selective, her aunt would say. But they'd never actually made it to a bed, she recalled with a chuckle. Then her breath caught thinking what he could do if he really had time and space to get his groove on. Oh, boy. She wasn't sure she could live through that kind of pleasure and not come out forever changed on the other side.

Come to think of it, she wasn't sure she hadn't already been altered on a fundamental level. Could one encounter with the wolf have ruined her for all other men? It frightened her a little to think that it just might be possible.

Shoving such disturbing thoughts from her mind with deliberate intent, she focused on the task at hand. She had enough clothes for Zach. She packed most of them, leaving one set out for him to wear now. Then she started in on her outfits, packing what she could as she went along.

Frustrated by her inability to find a particular knit top she was looking for, she retreated down the stairs into the small laundry room off the kitchen. There it was. On top of a basket of clean laundry she hadn't had time to sort and fold and bring upstairs.

She was bent over the basket when she suddenly felt Jesse at her back. He gave her no warning before his big hands landed on her hips, drawing her back against him. Instantly, she was ready for more. What kind of drugging hold did this man have over her pleasure? She'd never been this randy before in her life. Never.

"Do we have time for this?" she asked, trying for playfulness instead of the true, greedy, neediness she was feeling.

"A quickie?" His tone dared her. "There's always time for a

quickie. That's why they call it that." He chuckled and stilled her when she tried to turn in his hold. "Stay right there, beautiful." She went completely still, breathless, waiting for what he would do next. Anticipation made her wet. Or maybe it was just the way he ordered her around. She wouldn't have taken it from any other man but Jesse. That should tell her something, but she was too afraid to think it through. Too aroused.

Jesse slid his fingers under the elastic waistband of her shorts. Without so much as a by your leave, he whisked them down her legs along with her panties. Her knees began to tremble when his big, calloused palms shaped her ass. He slid one of his hands between her thighs while the other went to her shoulder, turning her slightly and pressing downward.

"Lean against the dryer." His words were almost a growl that turned her on even more.

She complied, knowing she was dripping wet, her pussy weeping for him, wanting what it had only had once before. She was still sore from that first possession, but already she wanted more.

She didn't have long to wait. He stepped close behind her, and without another word, he slid into her from behind.

It was a wild ride from beginning to glorious, breathtaking end. He pushed so hard, she came up against the cold metal of the dryer, but it felt so good. The contrast between his hot, hard body and the cold metal surface did something to her that she'd never experienced before. She started coming and kept coming until he finally joined her, long, agonizing, electrifying moments later.

They were both breathing hard again when he finished.

"Damn," was all she could get out at first, and she meant it as the deepest of compliments. "I guess I need another shower."

He pulled out and cursed under his breath. "We don't have time. Let me."

He reached into the clean laundry basket and snagged two towels. The smaller wash cloth he brought over to the sink that was next to the washer, wet it thoroughly and then wrung it out. He then returned to her side, crouching behind her. She hadn't found the energy to move yet and he took full advantage, wiping her folds thoroughly with the soft, cool, soothing cloth.

She yelped when he stuck a finger up inside her without warning, ostensibly to search out any remaining come. Most of it had trickled down her legs and he wiped it up with the clean corners of the cloth until she was moist, but with water, not with his come. He threw the wet towel into the sink and picked up the dry one, stroking over her skin until she was completely clean and dry.

He stood and lifted her shorts and panties as he went, redressing her in record time.

"There. Good as new."

"Actually, better," she said with a grin as she turned to face him.

He winked playfully and returned her smile. "I aim to please."

"Yes, you do, don't you?"

He bent down as something in the clean basket caught his eye. "Pack this," he said simply, handing her the gauzy broomstick skirt she sometimes wore.

She didn't really understand, but she saw no harm in taking it with her. It didn't need ironing and it was comfy for travel. She'd worn it on road trips before.

"Okay." She took the skirt from his fingers and clutched it to her middle, not knowing what else to say. There was so much running around in her mind, but so little she could actually speak aloud without sounding like a complete ninny.

He held her gaze for a long moment before the beep of his phone brought them both out of their daze. He was so potent, he made her forget herself. She was glad to see she had some of the same effect on him, even if it was a little inconvenient given the danger of their current situation.

He looked at the phone and took the call, walking out into the hallway as he answered. That was her cue to continue what she'd been doing before he so deliciously interrupted her with that quickie.

Now what was it she'd been doing?

They finally got on the road after checking the animals. There were no more stray shifters, thank goodness. Zach had used the time they'd spent packing in the house to rest and was able to walk with them into the woods that surrounded her property. They paused for Jesse to retrieve a giant camouflage bag out of the tree, then continued a short way to a big, dark SUV he'd parked near a back road.

Zach climbed into the back seat and promptly lay down, using the pillow and blanket Maria had brought with her from the house for him. He was asleep within minutes while Maria and Jesse worked silently to load and sort out the gear they'd brought with them.

When he put the cooler with the food on the front passenger side floor, she looked up at him in surprise. Where was she going to sit if he loaded up her side of the car?

"Bench seats, beautiful. You're going to straddle the middle, right next to me. I want to keep you close to me."

When he said it that way, with that deep growl in his voice, she couldn't refuse. The SUV was gigantic and there was plenty of room in front where he wanted her to sit. She didn't see the harm in it.

They set out on a back road that didn't connect with her place at all. Jesse had come in from behind the night before, stashing his vehicle in the woods. He'd trekked on foot all the way in through the woods surrounding her property, coming from a direction she never would have expected. By contrast, she'd heard those two idiots who'd tried to abduct her crunching gravel down her driveway. She remembered Jesse had called them the B Team, and she thought she understood a bit more about that now, seeing how he'd snuck up on her house completely unseen and unheard.

He was part of the A Team. Definitely. Thank goodness he was on her side.

She didn't want to ever meet up with someone of his skill and ability if they were gunning for her. Maria knew she wouldn't stand a chance.

They drove all morning, sticking to side roads though they drove more or less parallel to the interstate, heading west. As they drove, the clouds increased. Maria monitored the weather report from time to time on the radio. Severe weather alerts were springing up all over the place where they were heading, but there was no use for it. They had to drive into the teeth of the dragon.

"I wonder..." Maria sat up and reached for her pocketbook.

"What's up?" Jesse asked, instantly alert to her movement.

"There's something odd about this weather pattern. Is it okay to call my nona? She would probably know if a weather witch is at work here or if it's just nature being testy."

"Weather witch?" Jesse looked skeptical.

"That's what Nona calls them. Of course, she never had much formal training. She and my aunt are basically self-taught witches. They go their own way. Question is," she continued, "is it safe to call her? There's no way they could trace my call to get to her, is there?"

"I wouldn't think so. But just to be on the safe side, do you want to use my phone?"

"That would give you her number," she eyed him with humorous suspicion.

"Come on, babe. Don't you trust me?" The devilish smile he

gave her made her want to trust him with all kinds of things, but she was more wary when it came to her nona's safety.

Nona was old. She was strong in many ways, but Maria didn't want to be responsible for bringing a pack of wolves to her door. Or the *Venifucus*. Dammit.

Of the two options, she at least trusted that the wolves were on the right side of this conflict. Jesse hadn't tried to kill her, or abduct her. He'd screwed her senseless. Twice now. And he'd protected her from the bozos who'd broken into her kitchen. She'd talked with his brother and his brother's wife, who claimed to be a relation.

Unless this was some kind of insanely bizarre rouse, all in all, she thought she could trust him.

"Hand it over, sweet cheeks." She gave in with a roll of her eyes as he placed the state-of-the-art cell phone in her hand with a chuckle.

The screen lit up and she dialed her nona's number, wanting desperately all of a sudden to hear the reassuring voice of her grandmother on the other end. It rang. And rang. And rang.

"She's not answering." Worry made her brows knit as the call clicked over to voice mail. There was Nona's voice, but it was a hollow recording, not the rich sound Maria needed so badly to hear. She left a message for Nona to call as soon as possible and hung up.

"Maybe she didn't answer because she didn't recognize my number?" Jesse offered.

"No. She always answers if she can. And she always knows when I call, even if I'm not using a number she recognizes. It's part of her magic. She always knows who's on the other end." Maria thought through the possibilities. "She never leaves her phone home when she goes out. I called her cell number. She should have it with her. The only reason she wouldn't answer is if she's out of range of a tower or...something worse." Fear gripped her heart for a striking moment, but then dissipated. "But I'd know if something was really wrong with her. So would my aunt. We both knew when she fell and broke her hip. We both called 911 and got an ambulance to her within fifteen minutes. If something was really wrong, at least one of us would have picked up on it. Do you mind if I call my aunt?"

"Have at it," he invited.

Maria dialed her aunt's number and was relieved when her call was answered on the first ring. Her aunt had the same phone radar.

"Maria, where are you?" Her aunt's concerned voice was a balm to her senses.

"It's a long story. Are you okay? Why isn't Nona answering her phone?"

"She's heading for the hills, child," her aunt replied with a small trace of humor. "She got in her Jeep and started heading into the foothills as soon as the weather turned. I was going to go with her, but she said I had to stick around long enough to talk to you before I left reception range. I've been waiting for your call. As soon as I hang up with you, I'm outa here. I'm going to join Mom at the cabin and we're going to ride out the storm up there."

"Wow. The cabin? It's that serious?"

"Mom thinks so, and I'm inclined to agree. Someone powerful is messing with the weather. The weather—and a lot more—if my sixth sense is still reliable with all the lightning flying around. Mom says we need to go to our place of power. That's the cabin for us. For you..." Her aunt seemed to hesitate. "Mom said to tell you that your locus has changed. It's not a place anymore. It's a person. A man."

"You're joking." Maria's breathing slowed as the conversation got really serious, really fast. "How did she know?"

"How does she ever know anything?" A trace of her usual gaiety touched her aunt's voice. "I stopped questioning my mother's power when I was thirteen years old. So, was she right? Did you meet him yet?"

"I'm using his phone. At least I think it's him." Maria tried to be vague enough that Jesse wouldn't be able to follow her discussion.

"You do know weres have sharp hearing, don't you? I can hear every word your aunt is saying, sweetheart." A wolfish grin spread across his lips as he drew her attention with a caress of her thigh. "I like what she's saying. My wolf likes it even more. That means you'd better get used to me. I'm not letting you go anytime soon."

Her stomach felt like a herd of butterflies were suddenly having a fluttering contest. The molten look in his eyes almost made her forget she'd been on the phone until her aunt's voice brought her back.

"Is that him? He sounds yummy. Nice deep, powerful voice. I think I like him already. Hello, Maria's boyfriend!" she called into the phone, knowing Jesse could hear her.

"Hello, ma'am," he raised his voice only a little to be heard more clearly. "My name is Jesse Moore."

"Did I hear right? Did he say he was a werewolf?" Her aunt sounded more amused than alarmed, which helped settle Maria's sudden nerves.

"Yeah, he's a wolf all right. Look, we've got a little problem. Two men Jesse was trailing broke into my house last night and tried to abduct me. Jesse got there in time to help and his people took the bad guys into custody. They're being transported, as we speak, to Jesse's Pack in Wyoming. His brother is the Alpha." A low whistle was her aunt's only comment. "Jesse stayed behind because I refused to leave my animals. Turns out, there was a juvenile bear shifter in my care. His name is Zach and he was shot a few days ago. We're driving west right now, heading ultimately for Wyoming and Jesse's Pack, but we're going to stop for a bit just over the border to see if we can pick up the trail of the Zach's parents. They were captured at the same time he got shot. What can you tell me?"

"It all starts to make more sense now, I'm sorry to say. The weather magic has been building for a couple of days. It probably coincides with your bears being attacked. What kind of bears are they?"

"Grizzlies," Maria answered, wondering what that had to do with anything.

"This is bad, sweetie. Really bad. Grizzlies are among the most magical of weres in this part of the world. If these enemies are strong enough to trap two of them, we don't stand much of a chance against them. I can see why Mom bolted for the cabin."

"How do you know about weres? You never told me any of this. I had to find out the hard way," she griped a little, trying not to let her aunt's words frighten her.

"I dated a cougar once," her aunt answered rather flippantly. "Those weres are talented lovers. I hope your wolf is half as good as my cat was." The tone of her kooky aunt's voice implied things Maria didn't want to think about.

"Back to the weather?" Maria prompted impatiently.

"You're no fun," her aunt teased but managed to focus back on the matter at hand. "Mom thought they were building up to something. That's why the weather pattern is growing and not moving. It's localized over the area where they're preparing to do...well...something awful. Some kind of dark ritual. Stop the ritual and the weather will dissipate naturally. Let this continue and we could be looking at a hurricane-sized storm system covering the entire middle of the continent."

"Damn." The very idea shocked her. "What can we do?"

"Find the grizzlies. It sounds like everything started when they were abducted."

"That's our mission anyway. We're going to find their trail.

Help is coming, but we're the closest and Zach is the only witness. He's hurt, but he's healing fast and he can tell us how it all went down."

"Good. But keep that boy safe. The last thing you want is for the enemy to get even more magic under its control."

"They can do that?"

"From what Mom told me, yes. But only the most powerful of mages can drain magical energy from other beings. Only the most evil would do it from people he'd kidnapped. This is not good, Maria. You're going to have to be very careful. The merest hint of magic will be noticed by these people. You're going to have to track them the old-fashioned way. I hope your werewolf's nose is good."

Jesse stifled a quick laugh at her aunt's words. "I think he's up to it. He's an ex-soldier. Special Forces. I bet they taught him all kinds of non-magical tricks in the service."

"You're in good hands then." Her aunt's voice held a note of relief. "Tell him to keep you safe and when this is all over, Mom and I can't wait to meet him."

"No problem. Actually, you can tell Nona that Jesse's new sister-in-law is who sent him to help me. She thinks she's related to us through a common ancestor named Leonora who is—get this—a dryad. Have you ever heard such a thing? I mean, is it at all possible we could be descended from dryad magic?"

Her aunt didn't answer right away, and Maria's curiosity was piqued. "Stranger things have happened, Maria. Best we keep an open mind. I'll look forward to meeting this supposed relative and your new boyfriend once the storm passes. Be careful, sweetie, and take good care of each other. This is going to be a rough one."

"Take care of Nona and yourself too. Call me if you need me."

"I'd say the same, but there's no reception up at the cabin.

Still, if you're in desperate need, you know what to do." Her aunt's tone turned deadly serious.

"I remember. I love you. Give Nona my love too." A tear formed in her eye, but she fought it back. She had to be strong.

"We love you too, sweetie. Watch each other's backs and trust the man who holds your heart, Maria. This is your time. Your moment to decide what the rest of your life will hold. Grab it and make it do the right thing for you and for everyone who values the Light."

The call ended on that note, with Maria holding back tears and spending just a moment in worry about what would come next. Jesse put his arm around her shoulders and suddenly things didn't seem quite so dire anymore. They were together. He was strong. She could be strong with his help. Together, they could do what needed to be done.

Chapter Six

They drove back roads most of the day, stopping for gas once and making use of out-of-the-way public parks to have a picnic lunch and dinner. After full dark had fallen, Jesse turned off the road into a small motel that looked neat but rather run down. It was like something left over from the 1950s, but it would do.

"I know it's not the Ritz," he said softly as he shut off the ignition.

He'd run into the office and gotten a room at the far end of the long, single-story building. He'd then parked his vehicle over one space from the door. He could still see it, but it didn't block their door or obstruct his view from the front window or peephole in the door.

"It's all right. As long as it's clean and safe, we're good."

"It's as good as we're going to get tonight. I wanted to give Zach more time to heal before we tackle the recon. He managed to travel quite a ways before the humans captured him and drove him even farther away from the scene of the crime, bringing him to you."

"I run one of the only sanctuaries that provide free surgical care for the larger species of wild ones." She shrugged as if it was no big deal, but Jesse was impressed with her dedication to her work and the care she so clearly gave all of her patients.

"I meant to tell you before how much I like your place. You've got a good setup. Decent security for the animals, though the locks on the cages are a little problematic if you get another shifter by mistake. I could install a better security system for you when this is over."

"Really?" She looked so surprised, he had to lean down and kiss her.

"It's the least I can do. I'd do anything for you, sweetheart."

"Where are we?" came a plaintive voice from the back seat.

Zach was awake again. He'd been sleeping off and on all day. Each time he woke, he seemed to be in a bit better shape physically.

"We're at a motel about a half hour north of Lincoln, Nebraska," Jesse answered with a sigh. The kid had bad timing, but it couldn't be helped.

So much had happened in so short a time. He'd discovered the most amazing woman he'd ever met, and his wolf had gone ape shit the moment he'd gotten his first good whiff of her amazingly alluring scent. Jesse wasn't sure—since it had never happened before and Maria wasn't a wolf—but he suspected very strongly that he'd finally met his mate.

Now if only she could be convinced of that little fact. But she'd lived in the human world all her life. Although some of her relatives knew about magic, it was clear Maria had known next to nothing about shifters. He doubted she'd fully understand what it meant to mate one. It would be his task to teach her. Actually, it would be more like an honor. And a pleasure.

Jesse hadn't thought he'd ever find a woman who could claim both his heart and his soul so completely, but in the few hours he'd known Maria, he was already truly, fully and blissfully lost in her. The wolf wanted to rub against her at every opportunity and protect her with everything in him. The man wanted the same, though in different ways.

Jesse had seen the way she could take care of herself when he'd busted down her door and found she had already disabled two young, fit men. She was a very capable woman and he liked that about her. She was also delicate and feminine in a way many wolf women weren't. She might have trouble in the Pack because of that, but Jesse would clobber anyone who hassled his mate. He wouldn't give her up. He'd leave the Pack if he had to. He'd go anywhere to be with Maria. If that meant forsaking the Pack he'd grown up with, then so be it.

"Can we get fast food?" came a plaintive voice from the back of the vehicle.

Jesse shook off his troubling thoughts and got his mind back on the game at hand. They were in the parking lot in front of the motel. It appeared the kid in the backseat was feeling better. He'd spotted the familiar, glowing golden arches across the street and Jesse could hear Zach's stomach rumble.

"Let's get settled first. If everything is secure, we'll make a cheeseburger run, okay?"

"Okay." Zach sounded resigned, and Jesse took it as a good sign that he was on the mend.

"All right. This is how we're going to do this. You two stay in the vehicle. Maria, I want you to slide over here and be ready to drive if something goes wrong. I'm going to recon the room and as much of the area as I can while keeping you in sight. Lock the doors when I leave and sit tight. I'll be back in five minutes. If I haven't returned in exactly five minutes, take off. Drive and keep going."

While he talked, Jesse gestured for Maria to give him her cell phone. She handed it over with a raised eyebrow but didn't comment. He added a few numbers to her contacts list, set up some speed-dial options and then handed it back.

"My brother is speed-dial number one. My team leader is on number two. Use them if you need them, okay?" Jesse figured Maria was smart enough to know when the shit hit the fan she'd need help. She didn't disappoint him, nodding readily, even though her expression was troubled.

She followed his instructions, scooting under the steering wheel when he opened the driver's side door and got out. She touched his arm, drawing his attention, which he didn't like given their present vulnerability, but he couldn't deny her.

"Be careful, Jesse," she whispered.

For a moment—just a moment—he couldn't breathe. The worry on her face took his breath away. He leaned in and gave her a quick kiss, just because he had to. His feet refused to move before he showed her how much he appreciated her care and concern over his welfare.

He didn't know what to say to alleviate her anxiety, so he drew back and closed the door, holding her gaze. He hoped she'd understand the reassurance he didn't know how to put into words. He waited until she locked the doors and then melted into the shadows.

He had a job to do.

Thankfully, Jesse didn't find any threats either outside or inside the motel room. He went back to the vehicle four minutes and forty-five seconds later to find Maria nervously gripping the steering wheel, her eyes wide as she scanned the area. She was on her guard, which was good. But he still hated the reason for her wariness.

The danger was real, and it was Jesse's duty and fondest desire to end it, once and for all.

"The coast is clear for now," he reported as Maria opened the door. She tumbled out of the high vehicle while Jesse unloaded a few things they'd need that night, keeping one wary eye on their surroundings.

There were lots of trees to either side of the parking lot that provided some cover, but the lawn leading to the road left them very visible. By the same token, he'd be able to run over to the fast-food joint while still keeping the motel in sight. It was a risk, but he'd take this one, this time. His spidey sense—that indefinable thing in his makeup that always seemed to warn him when danger was imminent—was quiet for now. He figured it would be safe enough to get the kid some comfort food. Zach had been through a lot.

The least Jesse could do was give him a hot meal. And the werebear's healing body could use all the calories it could get. Healing burned fuel among all weres. Jesse understood that more than most. The kid would need a lot of food in the next days to help him get back to full strength.

They got settled in the motel and Jesse was able to get a dozen burgers and assorted other items for them to all share for dinner. He got fried chicken, salads, the ubiquitous French fries and drinks, carting it all back across the street in a couple of shopping bags. They'd be set for the night between that haul and the stuff they still had from Maria's house.

Jesse had claimed the bed closest to the door, taking the outside position should anyone try to enter through the door or the unit's single window, which was in front. The bathroom was in back and had no window, only a tiny vent to the outside up near the light fixture.

Zach got the other double bed, closest to the bathroom. There was no question in Jesse's mind that Maria would sleep with him, and he was glad when she didn't appear to question it either. The two double beds in the small room made for cramped accommodations, but it was the best they could do for now.

With another full night of bed rest, Zach would probably be much better in the morning as the poison slowly worked its way out of his system. He'd already been able to walk well on his own, having slept most of the day while they drove. Jesse had questioned the kid a few times about where they were headed, getting small details about the abduction and the location of his mad flight from the enemy out of Zach as gently as possible. Zach was proving to be stronger than Jesse would have guessed based on his age.

"I'd like to clean up if it's safe enough to shower," Maria said, breaking into his thoughts.

"Sure, go ahead."

She'd eaten a salad and some chicken for dinner, but both Zach and Jesse were still working on a few last cheeseburgers and fries. She looked tired and stressed, but she was holding up well, Jesse thought, proud of the way she'd been dealing with all the unexpected twists that had hit her in the last couple of hours. She was strong. Resilient like a willow bending with the wind. He really liked that about her.

She slipped into the small bathroom and he heard the shower go on. Zach ate steadily, as did Jesse. Both of them knew food was important to fuel a shifter's strength and stamina. They had naturally high metabolisms, necessary to power their special abilities.

"Are you thinking of mating her?" Zach asked, sounding more like a judgmental adult than the young teen he still was. "She's only human. Not a good match, my parents would say."

"Your parents—and you—are wrong, Zach." Jesse had to stand up to the boy's derisive comment. The kid had to know who was Alpha here. Sure, the bear might be more magical, and in time, Zach might grow into an Alpha to be rivaled, but for now he was still just a hurt kid, bear or not. The wolf was in charge of this little mission and it was time the kid understood that once and for all.

Zach bristled, but Jesse went on. "The doc descends from a magic even more powerful than yours or mine. She is the granddaughter of the dryad Leonora. I was sent to bring her back to Wyoming, to meet her grandmother." Zach didn't need to know the details of Leonora's injury or the need for them to gather all her relatives so she could be freed from the tree that kept her body safe and healed. "In fact, my brother just mated another of Leonora's granddaughters, a former police detective named Sally. Turns out, she's also descended from Rothgar the Great and Neveril the Mighty. You've heard of them, haven't you?"

Zach nodded grudgingly. "But their legend is ancient. I heard your brother's mate can't even shift."

"Maybe not, but the forest speaks to her. She is a true daughter of the dryad, with a little bit of famous wolf blood and the courage to match. I've seen her in action, Zach. She's Alpha through and through. The Pack loves her already, and I think you probably know enough about wolves to realize that we don't usually accept outsiders easily or well. Especially as mate to the Alpha."

Zach looked suspicious but thoughtful as he polished off another cheeseburger, but he held his tongue. Good. He was learning. Thinking. Not mouthing off anymore. It was a step in the right direction.

"There's something else you should know," Jesse said in a quiet voice. He was about to tell something to the youngster that wasn't general knowledge except among certain Alphas and the Lords of all *Were*. "Have you heard anything about a group of ex-military shifters banding together and hiring out to do special jobs for other *were* Tribes, Packs and Clans?"

"The Wraiths, you mean?" Zach's eyes lit up.

Jesse had to smile. "Is that what they're calling us?"

"You mean you...?" Suspicion and dawning understanding lit Zach's expression.

"I was a Green Beret, son. During the last war, after my human counterparts lost the trail in the mountains of Afghanistan, they finally sent my unit in. There were a few of us shifters in the mix. We picked up the trail again." Jesse didn't have to say any more. Everyone knew how that had turned out. But only a very few in the shifter community knew some of their folk had been involved.

Shifters didn't normally go out into human society in such a visible way, but Jesse had always been a daredevil. It had been a game to hide his superior abilities from his human comrades. It had also been his honor to help the men of his unit—normal humans he'd come to respect and admire and call friend—when the need arose. Working with them had taught

Jesse not to underestimate humanity. They could be just as noble, dedicated, courageous and strong as a shifter when pressed. He'd learned to respect their strong hearts and the simple ability to fight evil without all the advantages of a shifter heritage.

The men he'd served with had fought on the side of Light in that foreign war, and he would never forget his comrades in arms. Every one of Jesse's current group of ex-military shifters felt the same. They'd learned important lessons that all shifters should know about humanity in those years they'd walked among humans.

"You're one of the Wraiths?" Zach asked in a quiet voice.

"I lead them, Zach. I'm Alpha of the small group of ex-Spec Ops soldiers who have found a home within my brother's Pack, though slightly separate from it. We're still adjusting to being out of the service and some of us have had a harder time with that than others." Damn. He hadn't meant to reveal so much, but for some reason, the rocky adjustment to Pack life had been on his mind more often lately. "I tell you this because you need to know that we're definitely going to find your parents, and I can and will keep you safe. And if push comes to shove, you need to follow my directives without question. I've trained most of my life for situations like this. You need to know not to question my decisions, my commands or my authority."

Zach sat back and stopped eating for a moment while he thought. Jesse was glad he was taking this so seriously. It could mean life or death if they found themselves in a bad situation.

"Uncle Rocky trusts you." Zach paused deliberately. "I believe you." That was some concession coming from a kid who'd been through hell. "Are the Wraiths going to help us?" An eager sort of hope lit Zach's eyes.

"You bet they are." Jesse had talked to his brother and some of his guys throughout the day while they'd been traveling. "They're coming, but they're on the other side of this storm." Jesse nodded toward the TV they'd tuned to the weather station but had kept mute. The image on the screen right now was of a massive circular storm system swirling on the radar just to their west.

The storm seemed centered over eastern Nebraska, with the bands of heavier weather expanding toward where they were now. In fact, while they'd eaten, rain had begun to fall outside. Jesse suspected it would only get worse from here.

"Uncle Rocky's coming too." Zach seemed to need to reassure himself.

"He is. He's en route, but he has to come overland. So do my men. Planes and choppers are grounded in and around the storm because of the high and unpredictable winds. Zach, you do realize there's nothing natural about that storm, right?"

"Yeah, I know. It doesn't feel right." Zach shivered.

"The weather forecasters are stymied. With no large source of open water, the storm system shouldn't be expanding like it is. And it's not moving. Wind should be carrying it across the country. This storm is stationary. We believe it's being generated by dark magic." Jesse and Maria had discussed some of this while Zach had been sleeping in the back of the SUV. Every phone call Jesse made or received that day only seemed to confirm their suspicions.

"Something to do with my parents?" Zach's expression was bleak for a moment before his mask of maturity came back into play.

"We think so. The Lords and their mate are working on it from their end. She is a priestess of the Lady and her mates protect her while she tries to penetrate the storm magically. So far, I haven't heard any positive results from that quarter. I just wanted to catch you up so you're not blindsided when we video chat—if that's still possible with all the electrical interference the storm is producing—with everyone in an hour. We set up a conference for eight o'clock. I want you to be part of it."

It would be much better, Jesse decided, to make the teen feel as if he was an integral part of the team working to find and free his parents. It wouldn't be good to have him feel like an outsider in something that affected him so deeply. He was a grizzly shifter with all the magic and brute strength that implied, even if he was still just a kid. If they didn't include him in the planning, Jesse was pretty certain the kid would go off on his own and it might be at just the wrong moment. Better to have him in on the plan from the beginning, playing with the rest of the team.

Zach nodded once, his chin wobbling a bit as he went back to eating his fries. Jesse pretended not to notice. Zach was trying to be strong for his family. That was all that mattered. He was maturing well beyond his years, and Jesse didn't want to do anything to impede that process right now. Zach could go back to being a kid when they got his parents out safely. Not before.

It was harsh, but that was the way of the shifter world. The human world too, when war and petty dictators screwed with people's lives. Jesse had seen that firsthand. The same thing happened among magic folk. It was time to give the kid a history lesson.

"You've heard of the *Venifucus*, right?" Jesse asked.

At just that moment, the bathroom door opened, releasing a torrent of woman-scented steam that made Jesse's wolf stand up and growl in appreciation.

Down boy.

"That's the group who sent those guys to my house," Maria commented as she came out of the bathroom. "The ones with the tattoos."

Damn. She looked good in fresh clothes—a shorts set that made Jesse's mouth water. But he had to keep his mind on business for now. Play could come later.

Though not tonight, he reminded himself. Not with the kid

in the room only a few feet away. Jesse would have to be satisfied with just holding her in his arms. He couldn't make love to her tonight.

Soon, though, he promised his wolf. As soon as he could arrange a bit of privacy. It didn't have to be *much* privacy. But some. The bare minimum.

That seemed to placate the wolf who receded and let the man think with his brain once more.

"Tattoos?" Zach asked as Maria joined them in the room, stowing some things in her bag before sitting on the room's only chair. Jesse and Zach were camped out on each of the beds, empty fast-food wrappers strewn around them.

Jesse held up his wrist and pointed. "Usually right here. Apparently, the *Venifucus* mark some of their minions with a magical brand that only a few people can see. My brother's mate can see them. As can her cousin, apparently." Jesse nodded toward Maria. "I'm told it looks like a stylized V in a circle with glyphs or runes written in the border formed by tight, concentric circles."

Maria nodded. "That's what I saw."

"Sally did too. She drew a sketch of it, and our ally, the Master Vampire of the region, confirmed he'd seen that before in the old days, when they last fought the *Venifucus*."

"My parents told me a little bit about the legends," Zach volunteered. "But I don't really know much."

"This is important, Zach. I'm afraid we're all going to know a lot more about ancient history before this is all said and done." Jesse took a sip of his soda before continuing. "There are two groups we need to be concerned with. The *Venifucus* and the *Altor Custodis*. The *Venifucus* actively supported Elspeth, Destroyer of Worlds, when she made her last bid for power and was banished to the farthest realms by the forces of Light. This was centuries ago, but there are some around who still remember that battle. Bloodletters, mostly. Our peoples were allied back then and worked together to defeat her and her minions."

"My parents say you can't trust the bloodsuckers. They're only out for themselves," Zach said with a hint of belligerence common in the young and foolish. Jesse let it slide, though he'd never have tolerated such insolence from anyone under his command. The kid had been through a lot and Jesse didn't want to traumatize him even more.

"Sorry to say, but your parents are wrong. There are a few who are like that, of course. There are bad apples in every barrel. But the Council of Masters have always been pledged to the Light. It's their job to keep their people in line. My brother's Pack is allied with Dmitri Belakov, a Master who remembers what it was like in the old days. Dmitri recently found his mate—a woman he's waited centuries for—and her computer software business employs a good portion of the youngsters in our Pack. We are allied on many levels now, but none so important as in the fight against those who seek to bring Elspeth back from her banishment."

"They're trying to bring the Destroyer back?" Zach was finally getting the seriousness of this problem. "That would take incredibly strong magic." Jesse could almost see the gears turning in Zach's mind. "Grizzlies are the most magical of the *were* Tribes. Do you think that's why they kidnapped my parents and tried to grab me?"

"I'm sorry, Zach, but yes, that's what I think." Jesse tried to deliver the bad news as gently as possible.

"I see." Zach swallowed and nodded, his strength returning as calmness descended. "And they tried to kidnap *her* too?" Zach had been mostly ignoring Maria all day, only talking to Jesse. He jerked his chin over at Maria now, as if she weren't already part of the conversation. It was insulting, but Jesse understood the kid's residual anger at being locked up.

"We're not sure what that was all about yet. I followed those two men from Wyoming where they'd been involved in the shooting of a young wolf girl and the kidnapping of a wolf boy who was later found strapped to a chair in a booby-trapped basement wearing an explosive vest. The idea was to kill as many of us as they could when we went in to rescue the boy." Jesse wasn't sugarcoating the information for Zach. "Those two men were either after the doc because she's also descended from powerful magic or, less likely, because they knew she'd taken you in."

"Why do you say that's less likely?" Maria asked, jumping on his statement. He hadn't shared his thoughts with her on this yet, but he'd had time to mull over the situation as they drove all day.

"First, if they just wanted Zach, it would have been easy to get him out of the cage without you knowing, despite the lock you had on the latch. That barn was too remote from your house for you to have realized he was gone until you went out to feed the animals the next morning. So they had to have a reason to come after you first. Heck, they might not have even known about Zach being on your property. If they'd simply wanted you out of the way so they could bang around your grounds without you hearing, they could've shot you through the window. Instead, they entered your house and grappled with you. They wanted to subdue you. Either that was for their own sick amusement..." Jesse didn't have to spell out the fact that they could have wanted to rape her. One raised eyebrow said it all. "Or they wanted to abduct you. I'm leaning toward abduction. We didn't find any of the men's footprints near the barn where Zach was being kept. They came onto your property and went straight for your house with only a cursory attempt at recon around the perimeter. I now believe they were after you, Maria."

She swallowed visibly and a hint of fear showed in her eyes.

"But you saved her," Zach interrupted, a certain superiority in his tone that implied he knew how the wimpy human had to be saved by the big, strong shifter. Damn. Had Jesse been as cocky and sure of his own magnificence when he was Zach's age? He hoped not.

"Actually, she saved herself. When I busted in her backdoor, Maria had one guy out cold on the floor of her kitchen and the other in a hold he couldn't get out of. She definitely saved herself." Jesse held Maria's gaze as he recounted her prowess, sharing a private smile of admiration and pure appreciation with her. He was charmed by the pink that showed on her cheeks as he complimented her ability to handle herself. "Nice work, Doc."

Maria said nothing as she lowered her eyes. The demure look was doing things to Jesse's libido. Things he couldn't act on with the kid in the room.

"But she's human," Zach objected, breaking the mood with a crash.

"Never underestimate humans," Jesse said sternly. "I've fought alongside human soldiers that would put some of our best fighters to shame. They are more than we think in our arrogance. But, as it happens, the doc is a little bit more than just human. She's got magical blood and healing hands. She's got the touch, Zach, and don't ever forget it."

"And a black belt in aikido," Maria commented from the sidelines, surprising Jesse. He'd guessed she'd had training but hadn't known about the level or style.

"Aikido? Really?" Jesse was impressed. "I knew an aikido master in the service. It's a fascinating fighting style."

"It's all about directing the flow of energy," she replied with a nod.

"No wonder you're so good at it. Healers sense energy flows more than others, from what I've heard." Jesse grinned at her, unreasonably proud of her skills and abilities.

Zach polished off another cheeseburger in three silent bites. He was keeping quiet on the subject of humans in general, and Maria in particular, which was a good sign as far

95

as Jesse was concerned. The kid was thinking about what he'd seen and heard, making more reasoned judgments than the base reactions he'd had in his bear form.

Maria glanced at the silent television and her eyes widened. "Is that the storm? Holy Mother..."

She grabbed the remote control that was on the dresser next to her and switched on the sound. The meteorologists were trying their best to explain something with science that was totally outside their experience, and not doing a great job of it. She turned the sound off again after a minute.

"We're heading right for the eye of the storm." Her troubled gaze sought Jesse's.

"In more ways than one," he confirmed. "Which is why—" he turned to Zach, "—you have to be as healed as we can get you. Will you let Maria take a look at your injuries?"

He didn't have to ask Maria if she would help the youngster. He knew without doubt that her heart was in the right place. She'd wanted to help Zach from the beginning when she thought he was simply a young bear.

Zach seemed to consider for a moment, then nodded. "She can help if she wants."

Grudging acceptance was all the kid was capable of at the moment, which was better than snarling opposition, so Jesse took it. Zach would unbend in time. Some things couldn't be rushed. Trust and respect had to be earned.

Maria knew her cue and stood, gathering the bag with the medical supplies before heading over to sit at Zach's side. The teen allowed her to remove the remaining bandages and inspect his wounds. As she laid her hands on him, Jesse felt the rise of her healing power. She was purging the wound of the remaining poison in a way that fascinated him. No healer he knew could do that when silver blocked their magic, but then, he didn't know any human-dryad healers. She took her hands away from Zach's arm a moment later, looking over her handiwork.

"You're in a lot better shape than I expected," she commented to Zach. "You could probably take a shower if you feel up to it. This one scab should probably be covered after it's washed, but judging by the rate at which you're healing, it'll probably be okay by tomorrow morning."

Zach perked up at mention of the shower. "I'd like to get clean," he said in as soft a voice as Jesse had so far heard from him.

Maria smiled at Zach. "Good. I packed some more sweats for you. Or you could try the T-shirt I picked up at the gas station. I also packed an old pair of jeans that might fit you."

"Sweats for tonight," Zach said decisively. "I'm still kind of stiff. But I'd be happier in the jeans tomorrow, if they fit."

"Okay." Maria patted Zach's knee as she stood, smiling.

She sorted through her bags and found the change of clothes for Zach, shooing him off to the bathroom while she reorganized her supplies. She spent a few minutes sorting and repacking her bags, segregating the dirty clothes from the clean in a way that amused Jesse. He just threw everything in one bag and was happy. Maria put a lot more effort into her packing. It was kind of cute.

"Come here, Doc," Jesse growled when she stood, looking at her bags with her hands on her hips. She glanced over her shoulder at him and smiled.

"Down, tiger. We don't have time for what you have in mind." Regardless, she walked toward him, her hips rolling in a way that made his mouth water.

"How do you know what I have in mind?" His hands went to her hips when she stopped in front of where he sat on the edge of the bed.

"I think I have a pretty good idea because—" she paused, licking her lips, "—I'm thinking it too."

He groaned, raising one hand up her spine, under her jersey shirt. He slipped his other hand down to the hem of her shorts, delving his fingers beneath, down the short distance to the elastic rim of her panties. A few more inches and he'd be able to feel her soft, wet heat. Already the fragrance of her arousal was driving him wild.

"Jesse..." She leaned forward, her loose, still-damp hair forming a little enclosure between their faces where only they existed.

Jesse silenced her words with his lips, denying any objection she might've voiced as he slid his finger under the elastic and found his way into her folds. She moved her legs apart and he knew he had her compliance. Her breathing quickened and he moved his other hand around to cup her breast, tugging the silky cup down under her shirt to reveal even silkier skin to his clandestine touch.

He felt her tremble as he reached his lower hand farther under her shorts. He slid his fingers in her slippery softness until he found the void and filled it. Two of his fingers entered the welcoming sheath he'd claimed too many hours before. The wolf wanted to claim her again. Rip their clothes off and lean her over the bed, the table, anywhere he could mount her hard and fast.

But the man knew there was another person present. A teen taking a shower in the bathroom only a few feet away. The rushing water masked any sounds they made for now, but they had little time to play this night. Duty had to come first. Duty to the teen, to Zach's parents, to the Pack and all weres. Duty to keep them all safe—especially the amazing woman in his arms. The wolf would not be happy until she was completely out of danger.

Only then would the wolf be satisfied.

Chapter Seven

Sweet Mother, what was he doing to her? Overnight, it seemed, Maria had become a wanton, craving this man's touch at every turn.

He plumbed her depths with his fingers as he claimed her mouth and squeezed her nipple with his other hand until she squeaked. It felt so good. Too good. Almost addictive.

She lost track of time and space. Nothing mattered but Jesse and what he was doing to her. Even so, she was surprised when her knees nearly collapsed under her when a hard, fast climax hit her like a wave. Her whole body shook and she moaned.

Jesse let go of her nipple and supported her quaking body, lending her his strength even as he continued to pump into her with his other hand, driving her higher. Oh, man. Nobody had ever made her come so fast. She strained against his hand, loving the way he mastered her body.

She lifted her mouth from his and rested her forehead against his while he strummed the end of the most glorious melody against her clit with his talented fingers. It was intimate, gazing at him in the moist cave formed by her hair. She swore she almost felt steam rising from her skin.

He removed his hand from her shorts as their eyes met and held.

"You drive me wild, wolf man," she whispered, feeling bold and sexy for the first time in a very, very long time. He'd given that to her. She owed him.

She tried to drop to her knees to give a little back, but his hand on her back stopped her.

"We can't," he cautioned her when she frowned at him.

"Why not?"

"Zach is probably finishing his shower. There isn't time."

Maria jerked upright. She'd forgotten all about the teen in the shower only a few feet and one closed door away. Heat flooded her cheeks and she knew she was probably bright red with embarrassment.

"Ohmigod," she whispered, stepping away from his supporting hand and trying to straighten her clothes at the same time.

Jesse laughed. The bastard actually laughed. She looked at him in consternation.

"What's so funny?"

"You, sweetheart," he had the balls to answer. She scowled at him, but he didn't seem affected by her death glare. "I love that I got you so hot and bothered that you forgot about the kid." His voice dropped down into that sexy low rumble that sent thrills down her spine and right to her clit. Damn. Even his voice made her want more of him.

"I wish I could forget about the kid," she muttered, running a hand through her hair. Dammit. Where was her hairbrush? And why was the damn hair dryer in the bathroom where she couldn't get at it? She was a wreck.

She didn't hear Jesse move, but she wasn't startled when his arms came around her from behind, tugging her back against his warm chest. She felt him kiss the crown of her head. It was a nice feeling, being with a man who was so tall and strong. She had never been with someone like Jesse. When they parted, she suspected she would probably be a wreck. But that was a problem for another time.

"You're cute when you're flustered, Doc." He swayed back and forth with her in his embrace, comforting her.

"I don't know how you can be so nice," she mumbled against his arm. "I got my cookie, but you got left holding the bag. I wanted to make it up to you, but you said we didn't have time," she reminded him.

"And we don't have time. Not for what I want to do to you, babe." He pulled her backside into the hard ridge of his cock, rubbing lightly. "I want you, Maria."

"Oh, Jesse..." She tried to turn in his arms, but he wouldn't allow it. Resigned, she stayed where she was.

"It's okay, sweetheart. I'll survive. It's not exactly comfortable, but I've dealt with worse in my life."

The slight hitch in his voice led her to believe he probably had been subject to far worse. His calming words and reassuring touch made her feel a little better and not quite so self-conscious.

"I'm sorry, Jesse." She stroked his forearm, which was resting around her middle. He was just so big that he made her feel petite by comparison. Petite and protected.

They stood there, facing the television, spooning while standing up until the door to the bathroom opened. The cloud of soap-scented steam that came out of the small room would hopefully mask any trace of their intimacy to sensitive *were* noses. Maria had become very conscious of the fact that neither of her companions were human. Both had senses and abilities that were well beyond the scope of mere human experience.

Jesse released her and Maria moved to help Zach. Only one of his injuries needed a new bandage for the night. It had scabbed over, but it would be better if it was protected while he slept.

When that was done, they cleaned up the debris from their meal and set up the computer for their scheduled video chat. Jesse had set all their phones to charge while eating, so everything with a battery would be fully charged when they were ready to go tomorrow morning.

Maria stayed in the background during the video exchange, listening with grim attention to everything they'd learned and where all the players were. The storm was interfering big time—both in mundane terms and magically.

Maria could see two video chat boxes open on the laptop screen. One contained Jason and Sally. The other held two identical men and a gorgeous blonde woman. They must be the *Lords* Jesse kept referring to. The woman was apparently their wife, Allie. Maria made a note to ask about *that* relationship if she ever worked up the nerve. Allie was also some kind of priestess.

The woman claimed the storm was interfering with her attempts to scry. Maria assumed that was some kind of magical location spell. Nobody on the other end of the chat was any closer to locating exactly where Zach's parents were being held, except for the general area of the eye of the very unnatural storm.

It became apparent to Maria that Sally was using her detective skills to try to track down leads on Zach's parents the mundane way while Allie was using magic. Neither was making any real progress, but they both still vowed to continue working on the problem.

One thing became clear to Maria while she watched the men discuss their options. First, the men on the screen both loved and respected the women with them. It wasn't quite what Maria had expected. Ever since she'd first discovered weres existed, she figured the males would rule over the females with an iron fist. That distorted view probably came from her first shifter encounter—a female cougar who'd been abused by the man she was with. Maria had just assumed the man had been another shifter, but seeing how these males listened to the women with them as equals, she wasn't so sure.

By the time they wrapped up the video chat close to an hour later, Maria couldn't stop yawning. Not that the discussion had been boring. On the contrary, she'd learned all kinds of interesting things just by listening to the conversation. Still, it had been a very long day and it was catching up with her.

When the conference ended, Maria climbed under the covers and gave in to her exhaustion. Zach settled in the other bed as well. Only Jesse stayed up, working on the computer and occasionally watching the television screen that showed the expanding circumference of the storm.

Jesse called Zach's uncle, Rocky, and talked with him for a while before handing the phone over to Zach. At that point, Maria could barely keep her eyes open. The clipped conversation of facts and data that had taken place between Rocky and Jesse turned into one of reassurance and soft words when the uncle talked with his nephew.

They were still on the phone when Maria drifted off. She roused for just a moment sometime later when Jesse's strong body spooned her from behind. Having someone in bed with her wasn't a common occurrence for her, but it felt perfectly natural and incredibly comforting. She fell back asleep with his arms around her and didn't know anything more until morning.

Maria woke sometime around dawn the next day. It took her a moment to remember where she was and everything that had transpired the day before. She heard rain pouring down outside, and when she opened her eyes, she found Jesse sitting at the single desk where he'd set up the computer the night before. He had what looked like real estate records up on the screen, followed by a map.

Zach was in the bathroom, judging by the empty bed and closed door. Maria stretched and yawned, coming awake slowly. She'd slept remarkably well for being in a strange place, in a strange bed and with a really strange—in a good way—man holding her in his arms all night long. She felt warm and fuzzy just thinking about that. Never in her life had she felt so safe and sort of...cherished was a good word for it, she thought.

Jesse just made her feel really special. So few men had ever done that for her. He really was one of a kind in many different ways. She wondered idly if it was something common to shifter men or if it was something unique to Jesse.

"Your cousin is a genius," he said out of the blue. She'd thought she was being really quiet, but he must've realized she'd been awake for the past few minutes. And she knew darn well she'd been staring at his muscular back, so well defined in a well-worn, olive-green T-shirt.

His words caught her attention and she crawled toward the end of the bed so she could look over his shoulder and try to see more of what he was looking at on the screen. Definitely real estate records. There was a series of photos of a very impressive home.

"What did she find?"

"The epicenter. The house where Zach's parents are most likely being kept."

"Are you sure? How did she narrow it down? How can you be sure that's the place?" She struggled free of the covers and sat on the edge of the bed, wide awake now, looking at the images on the screen.

"She used the eye of the storm to start her search, then got her computer geeks to hack into real estate records in that area. The Lords and the Master Vampire and his resources worked with Sally, combining intel, and she came up with this estate. Turns out, one of the bloodletters has been watching this place for some time now. They've got long memories—some of those guys are downright ancient—and they've kept a watch on the *Venifucus* over the years way more than any of our kind."

"Bloodletters? You mean like vampires, right?" She felt stupid saying it, but she wanted to be sure she understood the lexicon in this strange new world she'd just encountered.

"Vamps, yes." Jesse grinned over his shoulder at her. "Sharp teeth, they drink blood, burn in the sun. Like in the movies. Well, not all the movies. There are a lot of inaccuracies in human literature and film when it comes to most Others, but you've got the basic idea."

"So a vamp has been watching this house?" She gestured toward the picture on the screen that showed a very attractive living room that looked like it had been staged for a real estate ad.

"More than a house. This photo is of the carriage house. There's a mansion, several barns, formal gardens with a maze and outdoor pavilion, pool and pool house, tennis courts, helipad, landing strip for a small plane... You get the idea. This place is enormous. Many places to hide someone and lots of security. But yes, the bloodletter has been poking around this estate from time to time over the years. He'll be our best source of intel when we get there. Although, there is the question as to whether or not he can be trusted."

"Why wouldn't you trust him? He's helping, right?" Maria really didn't understand all the ins and outs of these magical creatures. She was discovering they had a whole secret society with all kinds of peculiar relationships and rules.

"Most of the Other races don't usually work together nowadays. We really haven't since the last time Elspeth threatened this realm. After she was defeated, we all sort of went our separate ways. Bloodletters are odd ducks at the best of times. They live so long. And if they don't find their mate, their sanity can be questionable. Depending on how old they are, they can stick to antiquated rules of behavior and customs. Some of them are just downright weird, but luckily, they mostly keep to themselves. They also like cities because humans are their natural prey. Weres, generally—with certain notable exceptions—keep to the country. We need open space to run and hunt. Cities are hard for most of our kind, though some do well there, I hear." He shrugged. "The different types of weres work together more than with other kinds of beings. There are exceptions to every rule, of course. Like the dryad, Leonora, who is friend and ally to my brother's Pack and lives on our lands. Although, she probably sees it as us living in her forest, but you get the idea. We have a couple of brown and black bear families and the occasional cougar, but mostly, wolves stick with wolves, cats with cats, bears with bears, and of course, vamps with vamps and magic users with magic users."

Maria shook her head. "This sounds complicated. And stupid. If this Destroyer woman is trying to come back and take over the world, you guys really need to start working together. Humanity won't stand a chance if you don't."

Jesse laughed. "Now you sound like my brother. He's more progressive than most of the old-time Alphas. He's rekindled the alliance between the Master who lives near our Pack and many Others. The Lords count on Jason since they've put out the edict that we need to form alliances with anyone on the side of Light. They use him to encourage the other Packs and send him to talk to other Clans and Tribes when necessary. He's become quite the alliance broker."

Maria heard the pride in his voice when he spoke of his brother's abilities. It was clear he loved his younger brother, but more than that, he was happy when Jason succeeded.

"That's good," Maria stood, needing something to do. She busied herself sorting through the clothes she would wear for the day.

If the Others—as Jesse called them—didn't protect the world from this Destroyer of Worlds, all people would suffer. Humans were unequipped to handle the kind of magic she'd seen so far, and she knew she hadn't seen much. Humanity would be totally blindsided. Most people didn't even know magic was real. They relegated it to the stuff of movies and books. Not real life. They wouldn't know what hit them if the shit really started hitting the fan.

Look how ill equipped they were to deal with the weirdness of the storm now covering most of the middle of the country. The weather people were increasingly stymied when she watched the television. Nobody knew what to think or how to describe what was happening. It didn't fit scientifically, though they kept trying to explain it that way. It never even occurred to them to realize it might be magic.

Or what it might imply. Danger. Not just from the storm, but from what was creating the storm and what might happen if the bad people calling up such violent weather succeeded in whatever they were building up to. Even Maria could tell that would be a seriously bad thing.

That's why she was gallivanting across the plains, trying to help Jesse stop them. There was a sense of urgency that was getting more intense as time went on. It had been a sort of annoying hum yesterday, but it had escalated to a buzz this morning. She'd felt this a few times before, but never quite so strongly.

"We have to go," she blurted out suddenly.

Jesse looked at her sharply. Their eyes met and held. She felt breathless. They had to leave soon. Something was coming. Jesse sniffed and cocked his head as if listening.

"What is it?" he finally asked.

"I don't know, but we have to go. Soon. Like within the next twenty minutes." She felt her spine start to vibrate and she knew she'd picked the right timing. "I've felt this before, but never so intensely. Please, Jesse. You have to believe me."

"I do, babe." He turned back to the computer and began shutting things down, much to her relief.

The bathroom door opened, and Zach walked out looking almost as good as new. He was wearing the jeans she'd scrounged for him and a T-shirt. He looked like any regular all-American teenager, just a bit larger than average. He was built on the big side and had more muscle mass than most kids, but not freakishly so. He'd fit in in a crowd. He just looked very athletic and tall.

"Pack up, sport," Jesse told him as he moved economically around the small room, gathering his things. "We're bugging out in fifteen minutes."

Without a word to Maria, Zach started packing the few

things he had. When he was finished with that task, he came over and started helping her without comment. Maria was kind of amazed the kid had unbent enough to help her. She had far more stuff than the men because she had a giant first aid kit and more clothes than the guys.

Between the three of them, they were ready to go in ten minutes. Jesse scouted outside before he loaded the SUV himself, telling Maria and Zach to stay put in the room until the vehicle was ready to go. When everything was organized to his satisfaction, he escorted Maria and Zach out quickly, with very little fuss.

They left the room as clean as they could—meaning they left as little trace of themselves and their identity in the unit as humanly possible. Maria guessed various kinds of Others might be able to tell more about who was in the room than regular humans. Weres could tell things by scent and would probably be able to say there had been two males and one female in the room. Magic users might have some kind of spell to show them who'd been there, though that might just be her imagination.

But there was a good chance the people on their trail were only human. In that case, they wouldn't be able to learn much from the little Maria and the guys left behind in the room. Just a bunch of fast-food wrappers and a mountain of dirty towels.

Jesse got behind the wheel and headed out of the parking lot at a reasonably fast pace, though not so speedy as to attract attention. When she expected him to head directly for the highway, he surprised her by turning in to the drive-thru lane at the fast-food joint across the way.

"What do you want for breakfast? We might not have time to stop much today, so it would be good to eat now," Jesse explained.

She looked over the menu board, surprised Jesse wasn't heading away from the area before stopping for food. She told him her selection and waited impatiently while Zach gave him a much bigger order and Jesse relayed it all over the microphone to the girl manning the drive-thru window.

He pulled the SUV around the corner of the restaurant slowly. Suddenly, she understood.

"You want to see who's on our trail," she accused in a quiet voice. "Isn't it a little foolhardy to stick around until they get here?"

"Hide in plain sight, babe. That's always best. We're not the droids they're looking for. We're merely a couple out for an early morning breakfast. Nothing to see here. Move along," he intoned like the storm trooper in that famous movie scene.

She had to chuckle despite the antsy feeling that buzzed up and down her spine. Whatever—whoever—was coming was getting really close. She shivered and rubbed her arms.

"I guess I see your point, but what if they spot us? I feel them coming, Jesse. They're almost here." Her teeth chattered as chills gripped her. It had never been this strong before and her reaction shocked her.

"If they see us, we'll deal with them. Zach is fit enough now to fight his way out if he has to, and I already know you're good in a fight. It'd be nice to clear the trail, in a way. Of course, if they don't spot us, we gain possibly valuable intel about exactly who is on our tail. Either way, we win."

Jesse pulled up to the window, paid the bill and began accepting bags of food through the window. As soon as the scent of bacon hit Maria's nose, her stomach growled. She was hungrier than she'd thought. Jesse winked at her as he handed the bags over with that little devilish smile that made her insides quiver.

Suddenly, her head turned as if drawn back toward the motel.

"They're here." Dread filled the pit of her stomach.

Jesse's smile widened. She had to wonder at his reaction. He almost looked as if he was enjoying this, and in a way, she guessed he was. He'd turned the tables on the hunters and had begun hunting them. Maria assumed a predator like Jesse wouldn't want to stay in the prey position long.

"Right on schedule," he muttered, grabbing the last bags of food and slowly passing them over to her. "Now let's see who we have here and how good they are."

He scanned the area while she focused in on the single car that drew her attention. It was sleek and black. A sports car built for speed.

"Bad vehicle choice," Jesse muttered.

"But it's fast," Zach pointed out from the back seat where he was staying low, just barely peeking over the top of the seats.

"Fast but not very maneuverable. If they had to follow me off road they wouldn't have a prayer. Stealing that vehicle was a pure vanity play. Foolish," Jesse scoffed.

"Stealing?" Maria repeated. "You think they stole that car?"

"You probably can't see it, but there are small scratches on the door where they popped the lock. Careless." Jesse shook his head as he moved the SUV out of the drive-thru lane. He parked behind a tree as if he were simply stopping to sort through the bags. A common enough task. He even busied his hands with some of the sandwiches in case anyone looked in their direction.

They sat watching as two men exited the shiny black sports car. One went into the office and came out a moment later, gesturing to the other. The men went unerringly to the room Maria and company had been in the night before. One faced outward, watching the surroundings while the other broke into the room.

"Those two are a joke," Jesse said in a disgusted tone. "There's got to be something else." He began to scan the area again while the two men disappeared into the motel room.

Maria felt chills creep down her spine and turned her attention to the woods on either side of the motel. She extended her senses, hoping that whatever it was that let her know things from time to time would kick in and allow her to help in some small way.

She opened the window a crack, following her instincts and needing a bit of fresh air. Information began to flow on the breeze and she reached out blindly to grab Jesse's arm.

"There are men in the woods. A lot of them," she whispered.

"How can she know that?" Zach groused in a low voice from the back seat.

"She's part dryad, kid." Jesse didn't look back as he answered, continuing to scan the woods. "The trees talk to her. Notice how she opened the window?"

"That's not why," Maria objected, not really sure why she was arguing the point. "I just wanted some fresh air."

"Anything you say, sweetheart," Jesse agreed in a tone that made her want to roll her eyes. He was humoring her. "What more can you tell me about the men in the woods?" Jesse's tone turned serious again and she let it go, focusing instead on the matter at hand.

"They're all on the other side of the road so far. Shadows. Men in black clothing. The metallic tang of weapons." She shut her eyes to better focus on the impressions she received—from exactly where she didn't know. "Oh, sweet Mother," she shook as she encountered something in the woods that made her skin crawl.

Her eyes shot open as she disconnected from whatever it was that had nearly caught her snooping.

"What?" Jesse turned to her, concerned, his hand covering hers on his arm.

She'd clutched him so hard she felt the tension in his arm under her hand. She released him, fearing she'd hurt him with her nails, but he didn't let her go far. He took her hand in both of his.

"There's...uh...someone magical in the woods with those

men. Someone...evil." She tried not to think how ridiculous she sounded. "They don't like him."

"Who doesn't like him? His men?" Jesse asked.

"Them too," she agreed. "But whatever is telling me about this stuff. It doesn't like him."

"The forest then," Jesse said confidently. "He's got to be pretty bad for the trees to dislike him."

She shut her eyes and focused again, listening to the information that was there when she allowed herself to hear it. She stepped more carefully this time, wary of the malevolent presence in the woods. She could almost see...

"He's hanging back, but he's in authority over the rest of the men. They defer to him. They're...afraid of him," she whispered as she received the impressions. "He wears a suit and fancy shoes. The others are all in black fatigues and boots. He's not armed, but he's even more dangerous than the fighters."

"Where is he?" Jesse asked. "Can you tell?"

"He's on the left side of the motel, near the back. The men in black boots have surrounded the motel, but they're waiting for something." She opened her eyes, looking to the spot where she knew the man in question was hiding, but she couldn't see anything out of place in the woods around the motel from this far away.

"They're probably waiting for a report from the dirtbags who went inside," Zach supplied from the back seat.

"Do you see anything?" Maria asked Jesse in a quiet voice.

"Moving shadows. Men in black fatigues, just like you said," he replied, concentrating on his observations. Maria felt reassured. She wasn't imagining things. "They're good, but not good enough for me not to see them when they move positions."

As she watched, the men who'd gone inside the motel room came out, holding a pillowcase that bulged. They'd taken something from the room, but she couldn't imagine what.

They'd only left trash behind. One of the men was on his cell phone. Maria shut her eyes again to concentrate on the information that was there if she really listened.

"The man in the suit in the woods is on the phone. He's talking to the guy in front of the motel. He's yelling at him and cursing," she reported. Where she was getting this information from, she had no idea. She hoped she wasn't making it up, but she didn't think she was.

"That makes sense," Zach whispered with a trace of humor in his voice. "The dude on the phone is wincing and looking kind of pale."

"Suit man is not happy. He just threw his phone against a tree. It smashed. He's stomping away, seething. He's heading away from the motel. He's going to a side road behind the motel. He left his car on the side of the road. It's shiny. Silver. Sleek. It's a cat. A Jaguar." Maria opened her eyes, amazed at the detail of the information she was able to pick up. It had never been quite like this before.

"Figures," Jesse said with a trace of humor. "Damn felines."

Zach chuckled from the back seat. "Says the canine."

"The team is pulling back," Jesse reported, scanning the woods. Maria saw the two men who'd broken into the motel room get back into their car. The pillowcase went into the back seat of their stolen black sports car.

Jesse bit into one of the breakfast sandwiches, looking for all the world like a guy who'd just stopped for a snack. He handed one to Maria casually.

"Eat up," he said with a friendly smile. "Just in case anybody's looking. It also couldn't hurt to feed the beast." He grinned at her as her stomach growled again.

She leaned forward playfully and took a big bite of the sandwich in his hand, holding his gaze. She licked her lips and things went from playful to sinful in a heartbeat. She chewed, held captive by his gaze, starving for his touch.

"Jeez, guys. Get a room already," Zach groused from behind them, startling Maria out of the dreamlike state she'd been in.

The teenager stuck his hand over the seat, right between Maria and Jesse to grab another of the bags that held food. He dumped it out on the back seat and began munching on whatever came to hand. Maria was surprised at how fast the kid could pack it away. Even more so than other teenage boys she'd been around.

Maria turned back to her study of the motel. The black sports car was gone. Closing her eyes, she knew the silver Jaguar was gone as well. The team of soldiers was almost gone. One paused—the last one out—to scratch something into a tree and drop something white on the ground, which he then kicked debris over hastily before running to catch up with his group. They too had left large black SUVs parked on that back road. They all piled into the vehicles and followed after the Jaguar at a less speedy pace.

"One of the soldiers left something," Maria reported, opening her eyes. "Under the largest oak on the left side of the motel. He scratched a mark into the bark and kicked a note or something under the leaves at its base."

Jesse didn't say anything right away, though one of his eyebrows rose at her statement. He looked...intrigued.

Chapter Eight

"It could be a trap, of course," she stated the obvious.

"Hell, I was already thinking of trying to retrieve that smashed cell phone." He rubbed one hand over his hair in an absent gesture. "We might be able to learn something from it, even if it's a burn phone."

"A what?" She'd never heard that term before.

"A prepaid, disposable phone, activated under an alias, probably today, and meant for short-term use," Zach supplied between bites of his third breakfast sandwich. His words earned him a startled look from Maria and an expression on Jesse's face that looked like he was impressed.

"Do you think it's worth the risk?" Maria gestured with her eyes only toward the back seat. For her part, she was willing to take the risk, but did they dare put Zach in further danger?

"How far can you track the vehicles those guys left in?" Jesse asked her, making her tilt her head and think about it. She hadn't even considered...

"Gimme a sec." She closed her eyes and sent her thoughts outward to where that information waited.

She heard the sounds that painted pictures in her mind of three big, black SUVs following a silver Jaguar down a wooded lane. They went for miles down that road behind the motel before she caught up with them.

"All three big SUVs are still following the Jag. No stops. Nobody hopped out. Just driving at high speed. They're coming up on a cross road." She felt the car she was in start and begin to move, but she kept her eyes shut, focusing on the SUVs and the Jag. "They turned right, heading toward the highway. I can just barely see them now." She scrunched up her face, straining to follow, but for some reason, she lost their trail a few minutes later. "I can't see them anymore. They're a long way away, though. If we make this fast, they'll never make it back here in time to catch us."

She opened her eyes to realize the vehicle she was in had stopped on a road she recognized only from her inner visions. It was the road the bad guys had parked on.

"Close your eyes, sweetheart," Jesse growled in that low, sexy voice. "Tell me what waits in this forest."

Startled by the wording of his request, she nevertheless did as he asked. Shutting her eyes once more, she reached out her senses. The information came quicker and more easily each time she did this, she discovered. It was an ability she'd never really tried to use much before. Maria tried to see what was going on in the woods in the immediate vicinity and as far out as she could stretch her senses.

"I don't see anybody. Just the regular folk of the woodland. Squirrels, birds, a skunk off by the edge of the road. The men who were here before scared off anything bigger. The deer probably won't return for a while. That man's magic was foul and left a sort of gray miasma in his wake."

"That doesn't sound good," Zach said in a small voice. "Could he have left some kind of magical trap?"

"I don't think he had the time," Jesse answered calmly. Maria heard the confidence in his voice but wondered if he wasn't just projecting that for her sake.

"I could probably sense it better than you if he did," Zach observed in a brave voice. "I should probably go with you."

Jesse's eyes narrowed in thought before he turned his head to look at Zach. He just looked for a bit and then seemed to come to some kind of decision.

"Yeah, I think we should all go. The two of you together

probably have more magic sensing abilities than any Pack of wolves, but we've got to make this quick." Jesse began taking off his clothes. "I'm going furry. I can track better that way. Zach, you probably shouldn't shift yet. Maria, if you'd be kind enough to carry my clothes?"

Maria was surprised he'd want her along, but she sure didn't want to be left all alone in the truck waiting. She thought it was smart to involve Zach in this, to make him feel as if he were participating more fully in the rescue of his parents. The woods were clear. She knew that for a fact. And she had a sort of early warning system that always seemed to tell her if trouble was on the way. If something changed about their safety status, she'd rather be with the guys to tell them right away so they could all get out safely.

Jesse moved behind the door of the SUV, well hidden by the woods and the vehicle itself. He was there one moment, then a burst of magic stroked over Maria's skin like a caress and Jesse disappeared.

The wolf that bounded out from behind the door of the SUV was huge and brown and furry...and really fierce. Maria's heart rate sped up. He had the handles of a small, camo tote bag in his teeth as he walked up to her. She realized it was filled with his clothing. A T-shirt and pants, so he could shift back to human form while still under cover of the forest.

Maria took it from him and knew she was staring. She'd just never seen a wolf this big before. She'd worked with a few wolves during her veterinary career, but never one like this. He was gorgeous, and as he moved closer and stroked his face along her hand, inviting her touch, she felt the tingle of magic. He was amazing.

With a yip, he bounded away, clearly beckoning Zach and her to follow. The SUV was parked in the shade of a small grove of trees, well hidden from the road. It would be safe enough there, Maria thought.

When they entered the woods, Jesse went first, his nose to

the ground. Zach and Maria followed, her senses wide open to the sounds, sights and smells of the woodlands. It was quiet but returning slowly to normal after the shock of that suited man's evil power. It was interesting to watch the creatures of the forest and their reaction to the magical wolf and werebear.

The squirrels definitely noticed when Jesse and Zach passed, but they weren't panicked. It was more a silent respect as each little head lifted, watched the progress of the shifters for a moment and then went back to foraging. That's not what she would have expected, but it sort of made sense. The shifters, while they probably smelled different to the animals of the forest, they weren't hunting squirrels. One was tracking and one walked on two feet, hunting the trail of other two-footed predators.

Jesse stopped suddenly and Zach halted immediately. The wolf nodded to Zach and they were off again at a slower pace, Zach treading carefully. Jesse seemed to know exactly where he was going, following what Maria now recognized as the misty-gray trail of foul-feeling magic left behind by the suited man. It wasn't active magic, merely a sort of oily residue left by the man's presence. It wouldn't harm anything or anyone, but it wasn't exactly pleasant either. Which was probably why the forest creatures were waiting for it to dissipate more before they returned to their woodland homes.

Again, Jesse stopped Zach and went forward this time to meet him. Maria stopped a little behind them, looking around. She didn't sense any trouble, but as she looked more carefully, she recognized the tree. The one where the phone had smashed. She could see where the bark had been disturbed by the impact. Absently, she reached out to touch the tree and felt an immediate welcome from it like nothing she'd ever experienced before.

She gasped, but nobody seemed to notice. Zach was busy retrieving parts of the cell phone that Jesse uncovered for him. He stuffed the little bits of plastic and metal in a plastic bag he'd brought with him. Good thinking.

When Zach's little bag was full and Jesse's nose no doubt told him he'd found every last bit of the phone, they set off again, following the wolf. He paused again a minute later and the tingle of magic was all that warned Maria he was about to change back into his human form. She watched, awestruck at the sight. The amazing wolf shimmered and shifted, going to a half form that looked like something out of a horror movie—only worse—then to Jesse's familiar human form.

Human and completely naked. He smiled that devilish smile that charmed her so easily as he stalked forward, one hand held out to her. All Maria could do was stand there. She was frozen in place by the man and his magic.

She was more than a little disappointed when all he did was take the tote bag from her hands. She wanted so much more. Then she remembered where they were and why they were standing in the middle of a forest. And the teenager who stood by, waiting on them.

Horrified, she looked at Zach, but the kid wasn't paying any attention to her. He was studying a mark on a tree trunk that looked very familiar. It was the old oak that guarded the message.

Jesse, dressed now, moved in front of Zach and touched the subtle scratches in the bark. He then turned his gaze downward and kicked at some of the dead leaves near the base of the oak tree, uncovering the square of white, now stained with dirt. Rather than pick it up right away, Jesse paused to sniff at the air around the tree and a sort of grim smile came over his face. He bent and retrieved the square of paper, pocketing it so quickly, she barely saw it.

He didn't examine the note or speak again, merely led them away back toward the SUV. They'd accomplished their mission with minimum fuss and were back on the road before anyone spoke.

Jesse stuck to the back roads. Maria was pretty sure the man in the Jag and his followers had headed for the interstate. She couldn't be one hundred percent certain, of course, but she knew they'd at least headed in that direction for quite some ways before she lost track of them. They could have doubled back, but she trusted Jesse's skills to keep them as safe as possible. There were no guarantees. Their lives were on the line. But she knew Jesse would do his utmost to take care of them all.

"What kind of shifter was that who left you the note?" Zach asked Jesse after a while. When Maria looked back at him, he seemed truly puzzled.

"Never smelled jackal before, have you?" The ghost of a smile crossed Jesse's mouth. "They're not that common here in the States," he continued. "I met this particular guy overseas. His Pack origin was somewhere in Turkey, I believe, but he's a loner. A drifter. I'd heard he'd hired out as a merc, and that's probably how he ended up working with the *Venifucus*. He's a soldier. One of the best at covert ops. I knew his loyalties were questionable, but I never thought he'd go over to the dark side. He left his Pack to avoid that sort of thing, from what I understand."

"Golden jackals are very similar to wolves," Maria recalled. "They're all over Europe and Asia, I believe. Then there are two other kinds of jackals that stick mostly to Africa and aren't as similar to wolves as the golden. Right?" She looked to Jesse for confirmation.

"I guess so. I didn't ask too many questions because we aren't really allied with any of those Packs. But the guy I knew was very wolf-like when he shifted. In human form, he looked sort of bland. He could fit in with a lot of different cultures over there, and that made him really excellent at blending into whatever op he took on. He speaks a lot of languages too."

"What did his note say?" Zach asked.

Jesse pulled the stained paper from one of his pockets and

handed it back over the seat. Zach unfolded it and scowled at it for a minute before handing it back.

"What language is that?" the teen finally asked. "It's not runes or anything magical, but I don't recognize it at all."

Jesse glanced at the page and after a moment, grinned. "That's code, sport. It's an address and a message." Jesse handed the paper to Maria when he noticed the way she was leaning over to read it. "I'll have to double check to be positive, but I believe it's the same location Sally and my brother came up with, so I'd call this confirmation."

Maria looked at the scribbles, but like Zach, couldn't make heads or tails of them. She folded the paper and handed it back to Jesse. He pocketed it without comment.

"Do you trust him?" Maria asked.

Jesse shrugged. "I did at one time. Not sure I can now, except that he's never betrayed me or my men. He has his own code of honor, and that has led to difficulties with his Pack that ultimately made him go lone wolf. In this situation, if I'm trusting my gut, I'd have to say he's probably mixed up in something he didn't expect going in and is now stuck. I think we can take his information at face value but hold complete trust in reserve, if that's possible. I don't think he'd deliberately lead us into a trap, but he might not be in total control of this situation. In fact, I can guarantee he's not. He's only a hired merc. He's at the mercy of those who hold his contract and control the most magic."

"But he's still trying to help us. That has to say something in his favor," Maria found herself arguing for the jackal.

"True, but take it with a grain of salt. We don't know what's going on behind those walls." Jesse grimaced and seemed to firm his resolve. "But we will. Before this is all over, we'll know everything about what's happening on that estate. And we'll end it. Once and for all."

Maria was driving him crazy. Everything about her was attractive and made his wolf want to pounce on her. She'd handled herself so well that morning, tapping into her magic with little effort, not realizing how amazing she was. He'd make her understand, somehow. He'd show her in a million little ways how truly awesome he thought she was.

But they had to get to safety first. And solve the little problem of the *Venifucus* and two missing, highly magical bear shifters. And their misplaced cub, Zach.

The Mother of All had to be laughing at him right now. She'd led him to his mate and then thrown a few zillion complications at him, just to keep things interesting. Jesse was glad he could provide amusement for that complicated deity that ruled over his life and his people. He'd served Her all his life, but found She often delighted in making him prove his worth over and over.

He wasn't bitter, but in this situation, he would have preferred no worries, a private beach and a few months alone to savor the experience of being with the one woman who was meant for him. Jesse had honestly thought he'd never meet her. That there was nobody out there for him.

Thank the Lady, he'd been proven wrong. His perfect mate was sitting right next to him, trying to read a map as they sped along the back-country roads. Warm and womanly at his side. Damn, he liked the feeling of having her to protect and to make love to.

Speaking of which... She'd worn the skirt he'd asked her to wear, and every little swish of that soft fabric made him want to flip it up and take her right then and there. Only Zach's presence and the seriousness of their situation had kept him from bracing her against a tree and fucking her brains out when they'd been in the woods before.

Still, the idea of doing exactly that kept running through his mind until he thought he'd go mad. He had better find some kind of relief soon, or he wouldn't be able to control the wolf who clawed at his insides to get at its mate.

"We're running parallel to the interstate, but it's going to bottleneck by this waterway on the map," Maria reported, drawing his attention. She pointed to a bunch of squiggles on the map that he couldn't read the way she was bouncing the thing around. "If we stick to back roads, we'll have to go about an hour out of our way. We might want to chance the interstate."

"If they're watching the roads, they'll have both paths staked out. We'd have a better chance of slipping past on the interstate because there are a lot more people," Zach reasoned, impressing Jesse with his astute thought processes. "If they're waiting for us on that back-road crossing, we'd be sitting ducks."

"Interstate it is," Jesse agreed, pointing the SUV in the direction of the onramp. "We'll get on now so we're part of the regular flow of traffic. That's better than just appearing suddenly the exit before the crossing."

They were driving through farmland but Jesse knew they'd hit forest eventually. He'd be on the lookout for a big stand of trees. As soon as he saw that, he'd stop and let Maria's magic scout ahead. She might not believe it had to do with the presence of trees, but he knew how his new sister-in-law's magic worked, and Maria's had to be similar. Sally talked to the trees, much like Leonora. It might not be exactly the same for Maria, but Jesse was willing to bet that trees were the secret ingredient to Maria's sixth sense.

Jesse found what he was looking for about twenty minutes later. There was a rest stop just off the highway in a dense stand of woods. The small building had toilet facilities, snack machines, tourist brochures and a small strip of grass along the highway side to walk your dog, if you had one. There was also a set of picnic tables off to one side of the small building and plenty of parking.

The woods behind the building beckoned. Trees lined a

sloping hill, going upward. It was clear this was a wild space where people seldom ventured.

"Time for a pit stop," Jesse said as he stopped the SUV and unbuckled his seat belt. "Hold here for a minute while I scout around. See if you can sense anything, sweetheart," he said in a softer voice, wanting to encourage Maria to trust her abilities more.

She rolled down the window and shut her eyes. Jesse got out of the vehicle and threw Zach a gesture instructing him to watch over Maria while Jesse did recon. The kid was a bear shifter. He had magical skills most wolves couldn't match. And even if he was still growing, he was already stronger than most humans. Zach could handle himself if there was trouble, and Jesse wouldn't be far away. In fact, he wouldn't let the SUV out of his line of sight for a single moment. He'd parked in such a way as to allow him to see the vehicle from every vantage point.

Jesse did a quick prowl around, inhaling unobtrusively to take in all the scent information he could gather. No shifters had been through this way in a long time. Humans mostly. And nothing overtly magical.

He also evaluated those few travelers present at the rest stop in the traditional ways. He observed them with offhand glances that took in their appearance, their demeanor and the other subtle things that could be suspicious. Nobody looked overly interested in the SUV or in Jesse.

So far, so good.

Jesse gave the discrete signal that told Maria and Zach that it was clear for the moment. They got out of the SUV, stretching cramped limbs as they went. Zach hung back, escorting Maria to the rest room before altering course slightly to meet Jesse walking back down the wooded hill behind the building.

"How are you holding up?" Jesse asked the teen in a quiet tone.

Zach shrugged. "Better since you showed up, Alpha."

Wow. That was it. Right there. The single word that meant the teenager formally recognized Jesse's leadership and authority. It was a big step. Not one to be taken lightly.

Bears were a law unto themselves. Particularly grizzlies. Bigger and badder than most other shifters, they kept mostly to themselves. When they gave their friendship and loyalty, it was something special.

Jesse nodded, almost choked up a bit, but didn't let it show. "I'm glad," he said, and both of them knew he meant far more than the simple words.

"The doc said it felt safe here. She wanted me to tell you." Zach changed the subject, tucking his hands into his pockets and looking around at the nearby woods. "I sure would love a run."

"Me too," Jesse answered with a heartfelt sigh. "But it wouldn't be wise. Some magic users can sense shifting magic, and I bet you generate more magic than most. If they're on the lookout for it, they'll spot us."

"No kidding. Really?" Zach looked impressed by the idea. Jesse knew where he was coming from. Until a short while ago, Jesse never would have guessed anyone could track a shifter in such a way.

"So the Lords have warned. They've been doing a lot of research on our enemies since the attempt was made on their mate's life." Jesse grimaced, understanding a bit better now what the Lords had been through not too long ago. "We've got to lay low, even if it's relatively safe here. I had a sniff around up in the woods. No recent scents of note. Humans don't venture up there beyond the initial few trees." He looked up at the dense woods and Zach followed his gaze.

"Nothing but human scents down here by the washrooms," Zach reported, confirming Jesse's initial assessment. "No magic residue to speak of either. At least nothing I could feel. The doc either. However her senses work."

"The trees tell her things," Jesse reminded him. "Even if she doesn't quite realize it yet herself. Her cousin recently mated my brother and she speaks about hearing the song of the trees and the whisper of their leaves. It's pretty cool, actually."

"And you're not...upset, that your brother mated a woman who can't shift?" Zach seemed to scrounge around for words that wouldn't be quite as offensive as the first that probably jumped to his mind.

"Far from it. Sally's something special, and the Pack loves her. She's a hell of a woman and she'll make the Pack stronger. We all saw that almost right away."

Zach still looked skeptical.

"Do me a favor?" Jesse decided to leave that topic of contention for now. He had better things on his mind. He wanted a moment alone with Maria and this was probably the only opportunity they'd have for some time. It wasn't ideal, but it was as safe as things were going to get.

"What is it, Alpha?" Zach asked somewhat warily. Jesse liked that Zach gave him the respect of the title while still not agreeing to blindly follow. The kid was shrewd. And cautious. Perhaps more cautious than he'd been before his world had been turned upside down.

But Jesse was going to put things right or die trying. For the moment though, he needed some time alone with Maria.

"I want you to head back to the truck. Keep an eye on things and keep a low profile. I'm going to take a short walk with Maria."

"The doc? Why?" Suspicion laced his tone.

"You're probably old enough to understand this, Zach," Jesse answered plainly. "I just met her yesterday and we've been on the go ever since, but I know she's my mate."

"Does she know?" Zach looked concerned.

"Not yet, but she's definitely the one. The wolf keeps gnawing at me from the inside, if you know what I mean."

"Dad told me about it," Zach said in a low voice, appearing a little uncomfortable.

"Then he probably told you that mates need a lot of time alone when they first discover each other. I've been able to keep a lid on it because of the danger of our situation and the fact that she's not *were* and probably doesn't feel it as acutely as one of our women would. But the problem remains. I need to calm the wolf."

"No problem, Alpha. I'll hold down the fort."

"Stay with the SUV. Don't wander around down there. I'll keep the vehicle in sight at all times. We're just going for a stroll in the woods. No doubt her dryad side needs some communing with nature too, after all that time we've been cooped up in the car. Sorry you have to keep under wraps, but the less people who see you, the better right now."

"I understand." Both of them saw Maria walking toward them at the same moment. "I'll go down to the car and send her up this way."

"Thanks, sport. I'll remember this." Jesse clapped Zach on the back as he turned to go.

Maria spotted Jesse on the hill behind the small building that housed a few snack machines and the washrooms. It wasn't much of a rest stop, but it was good enough for a little break between all the driving they'd been doing. Her legs were cramped and walking up the hill felt good to her underused muscles. She'd been sitting too long. She needed a little stretch to work out the kinks. A walk was just the thing.

Zach passed her on the way down and actually gave her a smile as he told her he was going back to the car. Wonder of wonders. The kid was actually beginning to thaw toward her. Maria didn't understand exactly why, but she was glad of it. She hated that she'd kept him in a cage and couldn't apologize enough. She wanted his forgiveness badly, but knew she'd have to earn it.

She kept on up the hill until she met up with Jesse who was waiting for her, standing there looking so handsome she could jump his bones right then and there. The smile he gave her was downright sinful as he held out one hand in silent invitation. Knowing it might lead to trouble of the very best kind, she took it and followed where he led.

He walked farther into the dense woods, navigating a path only he could see through the large and small tree trunks and saplings. It was a beautiful place, filled with the loud silence of the forest. It spoke to her. Not in words, but in impressions. It seemed happy to see her and she was definitely glad to feel the untainted presence of the old trees looking after the younger ones and the little creatures that flitted among the boughs and scurried along the leafy ground.

She looked back once to realize they had full view of most of the rest stop, including a good vantage point from which to watch the vehicle. They'd be able to see right away if Zach needed help. She, for one, was glad of some time alone in the quiet woods. Maria wasn't used to having people around every minute of the day. She was more comfortable with animals out on her land in the sanctuary she had built for herself.

Zach was probably glad to get a break from her too. The teenager had warmed to her slightly over the past day, but she was afraid her mistake would always stand between them. She hoped not, but she was really afraid it would. She couldn't even begin to know how to make it up to him.

"He's safe enough for now," Jesse said near her ear. His warm breath on her skin sent an uncontrollable shiver down her spine. She turned to find him much closer than she'd expected. He was looking at her, but shifted his gaze to the SUV for a moment, no doubt having noticed the direction of her gaze. "I'll keep him in sight at all times, Maria. I promise." He held her hand as he took her a few steps farther into the dense woods. "I just thought we should have some time alone in this special place."

She looked around, noting the way the forest seemed to welcome them. "It is special, isn't it?" She looked upward at the small circle of trees he'd brought her to. They were between two of the largest of the trunks, surrounded by equally old trees forming a natural circle around a wide flat stone at the center. It seemed an odd formation, but as she listened, the power of her surroundings came through to her.

"A natural place of power," Jesse confirmed. "In ancient days, even humans would worship the Lady in circles like this all over the world. In modern times, most humans have forgotten about Her, but we haven't. We serve the Lady and are allied with all the forces of Light."

"I know about the Lady. My grandmother taught me Her ways, only we call her Mother Earth most of the time."

"Really?" He sounded both surprised and pleased. "That's good. That's really good." A smile came over his face. "So we follow the same religion."

She had to laugh. "I guess so. I've never really thought about it. Does it make a difference?"

"Not to me, but I've seen some of my men get involved with women who were really tied to their faiths. One of them had a bit of an issue with his mate about it and it keeps him from celebrating the sabbats with us. We miss him, and I know it bothers him, but he'd do anything for his mate. It's the way we're wired."

"Mate? You mean his wife, right? That's the same thing among shifters, isn't it?"

Maria had been curious about the distinction since she'd first spoken with the female cougar she'd known about the man who'd abused her so badly. She'd claimed he'd taken her to mate against her will, so he wasn't really her mate, but when pressed, she wouldn't say any more about him than that.

"A mate is so much more than a wife, Maria, as you will

come to understand." He moved closer, cupping her neck in one big palm as he lowered his head.

"Will I?" She found it hard to speak above a whisper. The woods stilled as if all of nature was holding its breath along with her.

"Yes, Maria. For you are my mate. My one and only."

His lips covered hers and she was lost in the moment. Something clicked into place inside her soul and she didn't need to question his statement. It was true. She felt it too. She belonged to him as much as he belonged to her. It was a relief to have him say it out in the open. A thrill to know he felt the same way.

She'd been fighting her attraction to Jesse from the moment they'd met. Fighting the intimacy that wanted to blossom between them, that grew into a closeness she'd never experienced with anyone else. She felt connected to him, and she knew if he left her tomorrow, a part of her soul would go with him. They were bonded now, and she would be hurt badly—maybe irreparably—if he left her.

But he'd said they were mates. That meant something among shifters. Something permanent. Binding.

Perhaps they weren't destined to part. Perhaps this amazing man could be hers. For keeps.

Maria fought to get closer to him as his mouth devoured hers. His hands were all over her, moving her, positioning her just the way he wanted her. He stepped forward, pushing her back, and she felt a tree behind her, supporting her. Welcoming her.

Jesse tore his lips away from hers as his hands went to the hem of her skirt. Both of them were breathing harshly as urgency rode them.

"Did you hear what I said, Maria?" Jesse's words came out in hot puffs of air against her throat as she strained against him. "You're my mate." He growled. Actually growled, from deep in his chest, and the sound went straight to her clit.

Oh, yeah.

"I heard," she agreed.

"You have no objection?" He didn't pause in his motion. His hands had lifted her skirt out of the way and were now working her panties downward, over her hips, with her full cooperation.

"Nope." She licked the salty skin of his neck and felt him shiver. Damn. She liked the way he responded to her—just on the edge of control. She wanted to see how far she could push him before he lost it.

She knew him well enough to trust that he would never hurt her. Not even in a frenzy would he allow harm of any kind to come to her. She trusted that as she trusted him, with everything she was and ever would be. It wasn't logical, but then again, who said love was ever logical. She paused, realizing the simple truth.

She loved him.

"Jesse?" Her panties were off, his pants were open and she needed him. Why was he waiting?

She stretched her neck to look upward, trying to find out what was preventing him from taking her right then and there. She followed his gaze and realized he was checking on Zach. Even in the midst of their mutual need, Jesse remembered his duty and checked the safety of his charge before seeing to his pleasure.

She couldn't see because her back was to the tree and it probably hid them both from casual view. Some people might be able to see Jesse, but not much of him and certainly not what he was doing. They were completely out in the open yet hidden. It felt supremely naughty to be fucking outside, with the sun high in the sky and people just a short distance away.

"I'm here, my heart," Jesse replied to her query, looking down to meet her gaze. "You accept that you're my mate and will be by my side through all that may come?"

The moment felt significant, and magic stirred gently against her exposed skin.

"I am your mate, Jesse." She felt the need to be formal here in this sacred space. "As you are mine."

His eyes smoldered as he held her gaze. He pushed inward with one strong, commanding stroke, joining them.

"I'm yours, for now and for always, Maria."

Words became both impossible and unnecessary as he began a fast, hard glide into her willing body. Breathless with wanting, need spiking with every thrust, she knew this had to be fast. For one thing, they couldn't leave Zach too long. For another, they hadn't been together in far too long. It had only been a few hours, but it felt like ages since she'd felt his possession. She needed it like she needed her next breath. She needed to belong to him and have him be hers alone for this short time out of time.

It was a physical necessity she had never experienced before, but she didn't question it. He was hers. She was his. They needed each other now. End of story.

Why that thought calmed her and thrilled her at the same time, she didn't quite understand yet, but she thought it probably had something to do with the mysterious way weres chose their mates. She would get the whole story on that score out of Jesse one way or another, but she had more pressing matters to attend to first.

Maria grabbed on to Jesse's shoulders as his pace increased. He pounded into her, but the tree against her back was as comfortable as a bed, giving her support and even...encouragement? Since when did trees do anything of the kind?

She pushed the strange thought away as Jesse hitched her higher so that her feet were off the ground. He encouraged her to wrap her legs around his waist and she complied happily. The angle and depth of his penetration almost sent her to the moon right then and there, but he paced himself, bringing her with him, making her savor the moment as he prepared her for something...even better? She didn't know where the thought came from. The somewhat intuitive counsel came from all around. Somewhere outside herself that watched and knew and...blessed their union.

She was supported between the tree and Jesse. His head settled in the curve of her neck as he set up a drugging rhythm with his hips, his cock sliding in hard and fast as he drew them both toward the light that waited. The incredible explosion of feeling and passion that would bathe them in bliss.

When the climax hit, she felt Jesse's sharp teeth graze her neck and then bite down on the muscle that joined shoulder and neck. The momentary pain added something amazing to the blinding pleasure of the moment. She felt his body tense as she began to spasm around him in the most excruciating, exciting, exhilarating ecstasy she had ever known.

Something about this man, this place, this joining, was special on a very deep level. The pleasure engulfed her, burned her, wiped her away and remade her in that short space of time. No longer was she in her soul alone. A piece of Jesse was there, in the space where a piece of her soul had gone to join with his. They were one in a way she had never anticipated, never expected. Never even dreamed of.

"Wow."

Jesse chuckled at her whisper of heartfelt awe. Just that easy, she was brought back to earth. To the small circle of very old trees and the man who had taken her places she had never been before.

"Sorry if I hurt you. I didn't mean to bite." He licked the words against her shoulder, bathing the small wound he'd made with his tongue while his cock still pulsed gently inside her, reminding her of their closeness.

"I felt it, but it honestly didn't matter at the time," she

replied, breathless and feeling bone-meltingly satisfied after that amazing climax.

"Does it matter now?" He drew slightly away to meet her gaze.

"Oh, no, Jesse. That's not what I meant. Surely you can feel..." She didn't quite know how to put it into words. "We're joined. Nothing you could do to me is bad. You'd never allow yourself to harm me, just as I couldn't hurt you. The bite was good. Really good." She knew her cheeks were heating with a slight blush at the intimacy of talking to him while he was still inside her.

He'd made her more brazen since they'd become lovers, but she was still somewhat new at this level of intimacy. No man she'd been with before had encouraged pillow talk and few stuck around long enough to develop a really close relationship. She had pretty much resigned herself to living alone with only her animals for company when she started the sanctuary. Since then, she hadn't had a lot of amorous relationships. None, in fact.

Jesse was the first man she'd been with in years. And he'd be the last new man in her bed. The only man from now on. She knew that now. They were the next best thing to married. Their bond went even deeper than the legal tie of human marriage. They were mated in the way of his people. Joined together, soul to soul, magic to magic.

"I think I understand what my aunt was talking about now," she marveled, remembering those words she'd spoken on the phone about where her magic was centered now.

"Did she warn you about the big bad wolf?" He chuckled next to her ear as he lifted her off his cock, allowing her to straighten her legs but keeping her close.

She swatted his arm playfully. "No. She just said the locus of my magic had changed. I told her I thought it was with you, considering how close we'd gotten so quickly. Now I think she meant her words in a more permanent way. Our magic comingled a bit just now, and I imagine the bond will only grow stronger with time."

"Really?" He seemed truly interested in her words, even though he was again searching over her shoulder, making sure Zach and the SUV were still okay. "You can tell that sort of thing?"

"Sometimes," she confirmed as he stepped back slowly, as if it was hard for him to end their stolen moments together. "I'm not the world's greatest witch. My skills are small and mostly untrained despite my nona's best efforts. Until I met you, I've been mostly in denial about this other world. I was happy living in willful ignorance on my sanctuary."

"I'm sorry, honey." He paused, stroking her cheek with the back of his fingers. "I'd have spared you all this danger and intrigue if I could, but I wouldn't ever take back our meeting or this joining. This sacred circle witnessed our joining, and by the traditions of my people, we are mated for life now. I won't ever give you up. And if you still want to live in Iowa, I'll make it work. I'd give up my Pack for you. I'd give up anything, if only to have you in my life. I'm that serious about this. And about you." He leaned down to kiss her forehead, and she felt the impact of his words in the far reaches of her heart. He meant it, and that meant the world to her.

"I wouldn't ask that of you, Jesse. I don't expect you to cut ties with your family and friends because we're together." Doubt crept in. "Unless you think they won't accept me and you're talking about leaving your Pack because of that."

He hugged her in reassurance. "No, sweetheart. They'll love you. Some of the bitches might cause you grief in the beginning, but that's to be expected until you prove where you fit in the hierarchy. As magical as you are, and with those martial-arts skills, I don't think it'll take long before you settle their minds about where you fit in. And it doesn't hurt that your cousin is the new Alpha female of the Pack, regardless of the fact that she's not *were*."

He let her go and stepped farther back, helping her right her skirt. "Besides, I don't really live with the main Pack. I'm Alpha of my own group of ex-soldiers. We live on our own little mountain in my brother's domain."

"I see I'm going to have to learn a lot about shifter politics," Maria said, brushing her skirt into place. She needed to clean up but didn't want to break the spell of this special moment. This was, for all intents and purposes, her wedding. She wanted to savor it, rushed as it was.

"It's okay. I'll be your guide. As I hope you'll guide me when it comes time to meet your family." He smiled down at her and she couldn't help but smile back. She knew at least two of her relatives had already sensed much about her new beau. They'd given their preliminary blessing during that rushed phone call.

"Handsome as you are, Jesse, you'll have no problem charming two old women." She reached up and stroked his stubbly cheek with her palm, loving the tactile delight of his masculine features.

"You think I'm handsome?" His eyes danced with humor.

"Come on, Jesse. You know you are. A guy can't get to your age, looking as good as you do and not notice all the women panting after him. Which is at an end, right? Wolves are supposed to be loyal, aren't they?" Doubt crept in, though she tried to make light of her words.

"Loyal to a fault," he agreed solemnly. "Mating with you, Maria, means I'm physically incapable of messing around with another woman. I don't know how it is for you since you're not *were*, but I'll kill any man who touches you." She read the serious intent in his eyes and it made her shiver.

"I believe you. But you won't have to worry. I don't want anyone but you, Jesse."

"Good." Her words seemed to calm the beast that had risen to the fore so easily. "That's safer for all concerned."

She wanted to say more on the subject, but the sound of the forest changed and she knew their time in this idyllic place had come to an abrupt end.

"We have to go," she said in an urgent voice, reflecting the new tenor of the trees. "Something's happening. I think the storm is coming."

The clouds had been spreading all day, darkening and deepening. The early morning rain had stopped and faded into an overcast sky that hadn't produced any more rain. But she sensed that was all about to change.

Chapter Nine

Maria was right about the storm. A moment after they reached the SUV, the heavens opened up and rain gushed forth. Luckily, she'd had time to stop in the rest room and clean up a bit on the way.

She was fairly certain Zach had some inkling of what they'd been doing up in the woods, but she'd rather not advertise. She could only guess how sensitive a werebear's nose was and hoped she'd been able to wash enough to tone down the smells of what they'd done. Jesse had sniffed her when she came out of the ladies room and nodded, so she guessed she'd been good enough to pass the muster of a werewolf's nose. That would have to be good enough.

"I don't like this weather," Jesse said, watching the clouds as he pulled out of the rest stop and back onto the highway.

"I don't either, but aren't we getting awfully close by now?" she asked. "The sooner we find the source of this storm, the sooner we can stop it."

"Yeah, we're close. While you were in the bathroom, I checked in with my brother. They've got confirmation from the local bloodletter, and Dmitri vouches for the guy. That's as solid intel as we're going to get." Jesse's face was grim as he handled the SUV through increasingly difficult conditions. "Zach, your parents are still alive. We know where they are and we're going to get them out. My men are approaching from the other direction and should get there only minutes behind us, but every second counts."

"Are they okay?" Zach sounded understandably anxious.

"As near as the vamp can tell, their magic is being used to

power this storm against their will. It's not good for them right now, but they're still fighting. They're still alive, and where there's life, there's hope."

"Well, one good thing is that we know where we're going now and don't have to guess. Will the vampire help or is he strictly there as a lookout?" Maria asked, wanting to know more. This entire situation was so different from anything she'd ever dealt with before, but yet it seemed only natural to go riding into battle at Jesse's side.

Not that she expected him to just let her tag along. He'd probably tell her to stay with Zach in the car or something. She'd try to follow that directive, but she knew deep down she'd be too worried about him to stand idly by while he walked into the heart of the storm. Zach wouldn't sit still either while his parents were in danger.

And something about this situation called to her. On a magical level, she understood the power of the storm and felt it reaching out to her. The storm itself wasn't good or evil. It merely was. But it was susceptible to the control of strong magic, and right now it was being controlled in a malevolent way.

Something inside her told her she could change all that. She didn't quite know how, but when the time came, she would be ready. A lot of her magic was intuitive. She'd learned not to question her instincts. At the moment, every last one of them was screaming at her to seek out the heart of the storm with her mate.

Her mate. Just thinking those words caused a warm glow to spread through her body and brought a tiny hint of a smile to her face. Mother Earth had truly blessed her with the man She had sent in Her infinite wisdom.

Sure, they'd gotten off to a rocky start when he broke down her door in the middle of the night, but he'd been making it up to her ever since. Making it up in the most delicious, delectable, delightful ways...

"The vamp is an unknown quantity to me. I've heard of him but never worked with him directly. Dmitri says he's a bit of a recluse, even among his own kind. He's very old. Ancient, in fact. His name is Marco and we speculate he goes back to the time of the Roman Empire."

"Seriously?" Maria was impressed. "That's pretty cool."

"Being an ancient means he's very good at what he does. By the time a bloodletter has a couple of centuries on him, usually he's gained a level of control over his abilities the younger ones lack. If he makes it to the five-hundred-year mark, he's got both skill and control. Those who are older than that are usually either Masters or hermits. This one is among the latter, at least in recent memory. Dmitri fought alongside this guy the last time the *Venifucus* threatened our realm, which says a lot for the kind of man he was back then. What he is now? I really can't say until we get to know each other better."

Jesse's eyes were constantly moving as he drove through the downpour. She assumed he was talking more for her and Zach's benefit than because he suddenly had become chatty. And it was working. His running narrative was definitely helping keep her mind off the storm and the treacherous conditions through which he drove.

The sky was dark green in spots and the clouds were so dense and gray that Maria couldn't tell if it was day or night. She wondered if the vampire was limited by the position of the sun regardless of the weather conditions. She knew so little about this world, really. There was going to be a lot to learn...if they lived through this little adventure.

The estate where Zach's parents were being held was large, which could work to his advantage, Jesse thought as he drove through the increasing storm. Getting in would be relatively easy, but traversing the ground to get to the captive grizzlies was another thing entirely. The cavalry was on its way, but the bears didn't have a lot of time, judging from the building intensity of the storm.

It was growing fast now, as if the bears had held out as long as they could. Jesse had to act now, but how could he with Maria and Zach in tow? He doubted either one of them would stay put if he told them to hang back. And being a realist, he had to admit he admired them both for it.

It was Zach's right to help defend his family. Even as a teenager, the boy had serious power of his own that was not to be scorned. And even though he didn't know all there was to know yet about his new mate, Jesse had seen a little bit of what Maria could do against human opponents. The more he was around her, the more her magical senses seemed to ignite. She was more powerful than she realized.

He exited the highway slightly before the road that would take him to the estate. The note from his jackal friend had said the direct routes were being watched. The back roads would work just as well and allow him to meet up with the one ace they had up their sleeve. The bloodletter.

Ancient as he was, Marco could operate in the hours before sunset as long as the sun was obliterated by heavy clouds. Jesse looked up through the windshield. Clouds didn't get much heavier than this.

Jesse followed the directions Jason had given him to the outskirts of the massive estate. It probably should be called a ranch, but there were no animals on the land and the farmland had been allowed to become forest over the past century or two. That might count in their favor considering Maria's dryad heritage.

He pulled the SUV over in a copse of trees, protected somewhat from the whipping wind and rain by their leafy bower. The canopy of leaves was swinging wildly in the pale-greenish light of what was left of the day, but underneath the dense roof of leaves and branches, it was a bit quieter.

Jesse cracked a window, and immediately Maria covered her ears with her hands.

"What?" he demanded, rolling the window back up. "What is it?"

"Sorry. They're screaming. Frightened," she sputtered, truly shocked by whatever she'd just experienced.

"My parents?" Zach asked worriedly from behind them.

"No. The trees. The forest. They don't like what's happening. It's...evil, I guess is the best word. They're angry and the younger ones are afraid."

Maria looked out her window and jumped back about six inches, straight into Jesse's arms. He looked past her to see what had frightened her and found a stranger's face peering into the passenger side window. Despite the maelstrom around him, his appearance was untouched by the wind or rain.

It had to be the vampire.

"Marco?" Jesse asked, knowing the bloodletter's hearing was as good as his own.

The man nodded. "And you're Jesse Moore. I've been told to tell you that Rocky is almost here. His ETA is about twenty minutes. And your brother sends his regards. Bravo kilo X-ray."

There it was, the code Jason had set up. This was indeed Marco. Jesse thought hard about his next move. These guys had to be invited in, or so the story went. Did he dare expose Zach and Maria to the vampire at close range? He didn't see that he had any other choice.

"Would you like to come inside?"

Marco bowed his head to the side in a very old-world motion, indicating he would.

"Zach, move over behind me," Jesse instructed the teen carefully. The next moments would prove whether Jesse had made a mistake or not.

Jesse popped the locks long enough for Marco to climb into the back seat. The rain did not come in with him. The bloodletter seemed to have his own little bubble of protection that didn't allow rain or wind to touch him. It was a neat trick and a pretty obvious use of magic Jesse had never seen before. Then again, he didn't know too many vamps reputed to be as old as Marco.

Marco began speaking almost as soon as he shut the door. "There's not much time to waste. The grizzlies are putting up a valiant fight, but we dare not wait too much longer."

"What's the situation?" Jesse was all business, glad Marco was being straightforward. Sometimes bloodletters didn't feel the same sense of urgency about things as folks who weren't immortal.

"They're being held in the outbuilding at the center of the storm. I was able to see them until the eye expanded. I dare not go there now, as it is calm and sunny at the disturbance's center." He shuddered but went on. "The building is a pavilion of sorts with a fire pit at its center under a circular opening in the roof. That's where the mage who drains the grizzlies and powers the storm has set up shop. She has been standing in the center of the fire pit, arms raised to the sky while she funnels the shifters' energies out of them and upward into the storm. I have seen this kind of magic before. Only once. Long ago." Marco's expression turned grim. "The owner of this estate is with her. I've been watching him for some time. When we get inside, he is mine to kill."

Maria gulped, but Jesse understood all about vengeance and this ancient vamp seemed to have a score to settle with the owner of the estate.

"He's yours. Does he wear thousand-dollar suits, drive a silver Jaguar and reek of expensive cologne?" Jesse asked on the off chance he was the same man who'd been stalking them at the motel.

"That sounds like him," the vampire agreed.

"I believe he has been on our trail. He had a group of hired mercenaries with him. One was once a friend of mine," Jesse admitted.

"Curious," came Marco's rather dry reply. "There is such a group inside the grounds. Shifters of many different kinds. I have never been clear about where their loyalties lie."

"Neither am I, though my friend did send us a warning," Jesse admitted, but as time was growing short, he forged ahead. "Do you know what this storm is all about?" Jesse checked his weapons, impatient to be off. He'd go in human form to better protect his mate and the teenager. Zach could go furry. He was probably stronger in his bear form anyway.

"The storm, if it is strong enough—magical enough—could cause a rift between realms. In this way, they hope to bring back the cursed Elspeth, Killer of Innocents." Jesse got the impression Marco would have spat had he been outdoors.

Jesse had never heard Elspeth referred to by that title, but he didn't have time to question it now. He was left with the fleeting impression that Marco might have some personal reason for his hatred of Elspeth and her followers, which suited Jesse just fine. It meant Marco would be firmly on Jesse's side in the coming battle.

"Is that why the forest is screaming?" Maria asked, still shaken.

Marco looked at her sharply, sniffing loudly. "You are of the woods?"

"She is untrained but descended from the dryad, Leonora. She knows only a little about her magic," Jesse answered for her, not liking the way the bloodletter's eyes focused on his mate. The wolf wanted to growl, but Jesse held himself in check as best he could. "She is my mate," he added for good measure, unable not to stake his claim.

"Understood," Marco answered quietly, sharing a nod with Jesse that spoke volumes. In his dark gaze, Jesse saw regret and what could have been sadness in the vampire's eyes, but it was gone so fast, Jesse couldn't be absolutely sure. "Come. We have much to do."

Marco opened the door and got out. Jesse watched Maria's reaction to the renewed noise from outside, but she was handling it better this time. They all piled out of the SUV, and Jesse noted Zach removing the outer layers of his clothing and throwing them back into the truck. He'd be freer to shift into his bear form when necessary if he wasn't encumbered by three layers of fabric.

Within a minute, they were on the move. The bloodletter had graciously extended his magical shield to cover all of them, and the protection from the wind and rain was much appreciated. Jesse thanked the vamp with a nod of respect, which Marco accepted courteously. So far, he was turning out to be a decent sort of fellow, but time would tell.

"I can shield your presence," Marco said softly as they began to move through the woods. "But only up to the edge of the eye. Where the sun shines, my power is moot."

"I understand." Frankly, it was more than Jesse could have hoped for. They'd be able to get very close to the objective clean. With two novices at stealth along for the ride, that was worth quite a bit.

"They tried to seed the woods with their evil magic, but the trees wouldn't stand for it. Many years ago, I spread oak and rowan saplings through this forest, and they've done their job well. No evil will grow where the oak stands guard and the rowan brings its blessing. Anything the trees missed, I took care of. I patrol this woodland every few weeks as part of my territory. I have known of the magic users who make their home here for some time and I have watched them and their ancestors for more than a century."

"Why?" Maria whispered as they moved as quickly as they could through the dense trees.

"The founder of their magical line was scum. He served

Elspeth and I killed him for it long ago. But his children were born innocent. They turned evil later, though they never had the ability to do much of anything until this generation. I watched, knowing sooner or later, one of them would try something."

That sounded ominous to Jesse, and he began to suspect the vampire knew how to hold a grudge for centuries if need be. Definitely not a man you wanted to piss off. Good thing he was on their side.

"I am thankful you are here now to aid us in freeing Zach's parents," Jesse said solemnly as they moved steadily forward under the vampire's protective shield.

Marco looked sharply at Zach. "I realized you were a bear, of course, but I didn't make the connection. The sun sets soon. If you three can hold off the storm maker long enough, I will do all in my power to assist your parents."

Zach seemed to weigh the vampire's words for a moment and then nodded. "Thank you. Our Clan will accept whatever assistance you can lend this night and we will not forget, Marco of the bloodletters."

Hmm. Now wasn't that interesting? Jesse marveled silently as Zach spoke formal words acknowledging a potential debt to the vamp for services rendered. The kid was smarter than Jesse had given him credit for being. Vampires loved formality. Most of the older ones had been born and raised in times much more formal than these and still held to those mores. Zach had done exactly the right thing, and Jesse silently applauded the teenager's intelligence.

Marco seemed impressed as well. "Thank you," he answered with a formal bow of his head as they moved along. "I will do what I can out here under cover of the storm until the sun sets. I can guide your backup to you when they arrive, including Rocky and the others I was told would be right behind you."

"My men will be on Rocky's heels," Jesse confirmed. "They're coming in from the west. Rocky comes from the north. They are mostly wolves, but there are a few cats and Others mixed in. They'll hit the ground ready to roll."

"Ah, yes, the infamous Wraiths. I am glad to finally meet their leader. When this is all over, I may have work for you and your men."

Jesse was surprised by the bloodletter's knowledge but didn't let it show. They were nearing the eye of the storm. Jesse could see a light ahead through the dense woods.

"How far?" he asked, motioning toward the light.

"Not far now," Marco answered. "I leave you at the edge of the woods. You will see the pavilion in the clearing. It is a huge structure. May the Lady bless your path from the trees to the building. I know not what awaits you there. I came in from above when the storm was still in its infancy and hiding the sun." He slowed his steps as the trees thinned and the light grew brighter. "Be wary now, dryad's daughter," he addressed Maria, making her jump at the strange title. "I am going to drop the shield from around you all when I go. It could be jarring."

"Thanks for the warning. And for the escort," Maria replied, remembering her manners.

"Brace yourself now," Marco warned. "I will drop the shield around you, lady, by small degrees, since you are unused to your magic."

Again, she thanked the vamp for his thoughtfulness. Jesse didn't like the small delay or the way the bloodsucker was eyeing his mate, but he also didn't want Maria to suffer from the sounds only she could hear from the forest. He watched her carefully as the vamp dropped his protection, noting the way her eyes scrunched and her hands made an abortive move toward her ears.

"Control it, lady," Marco advised. "Turn down the volume to a more manageable level. Imagine a control knob in your mind and turn it," he coached.

Jesse was glad to see relief cross her features as she followed the bloodletter's instructions.

The vampire left without another word, disappearing as silently as he'd come. Even Jesse was impressed with the man's stealth.

"This is awful," Jesse heard Maria mutter. She had one hand on her forehead, pressing hard as her eyes scrunched up in concentration. The winds were more subdued this deep in the forest and closer to the eye of the storm.

"What's going on?" Jesse asked.

"I'm seeing things. Getting impressions from the forest, I guess, of what's been happening in the pavilion. It can see the grounds around and it knows where the traps are." Her eyes popped open. "It's warning us. It knows why we're here and it will help as best it can."

"That's good, Maria. Really good," he touched her cheek, wanting to take some of the strain he read in her eyes away but not knowing how. "What are the trees telling you?"

"First, that they're really, really mad. But under the anger there's information. Older, calmer consciousnesses. They're showing me a path from the edge of the woods to a small maze of shrubs. There are predators in the shrubs. Four legs. Two legs. I think the trees are saying they're shifters."

"Cats or dogs?" Jesse asked, hoping the information the jackal had given him was correct.

"A canine leads the group, but he's not a wolf. Wolf-like. The others are a mix. Several big cats. A few mixed canines." Her eyes closed again as she concentrated.

"How many?" Jesse prompted.

"Eight. No more. The maze is the only way in that can't be seen clearly from the pavilion. They guard it," she reported.

"All right then." Jesse straightened and moved forward. "We make for the maze."

"What?" Both Maria and Zach asked at the same time. Both faces mirrored their astonishment, but Jesse knew something neither of them knew.

"Remember the message from my old friend? He's in the maze. If he was on the level, he and his men will let us through. They're mercs, not fanatics."

"Are you sure?" Maria's soft hand landed on his forearm.

"About ninety percent, but I'm going first. If there's trouble, I can take the jackal, and between Zach and I, the rest of them shouldn't be hard to handle. Right, Zach?" Jesse deliberately tried to boost the kid's confidence.

If this went south, it would be a lot harder to subdue eight full-grown shifters with only a teenaged grizzly and a human-trained woman at his side, no matter that she had a black belt in aikido. The only thing that gave him solace was the fact that his men and Rocky weren't far behind. The *Venifucus* fanatics would probably rather add Maria and Zach's magic to their storm. Even if Jesse were killed, they wouldn't have all that much time to harm his charges before the cavalry arrived.

They made their way around the perimeter of the woods to the spot where the ornamental maze was closest to the edge of the trees. They could see only the sloped roof of the pavilion above the tall, manicured shrubs and statuary. The sun was still shining through the massive eye of the storm, though low in the sky. The air was unnaturally still the closer they got to the pavilion and not a single bird chirped or insect buzzed. It was dead calm.

"The jackal waits just behind that small opening in the bushes," Maria said softly near his ear. When he shot her a surprised look, she explained. "The trees see from above. I know where most of the men are and I can see the grid of the maze. It's not very hard, and there are multiple entry and exit points. It's not a tricky maze, more for show than for getting lost in. And some of the statues are...I don't know exactly, but the trees don't like them."

"Bespelled," Zach added quietly from behind. "I can sniff them out if we get close enough to a trap."

"All right. This is how we're going to play it. Maria, you give me your best intel on the layout as we go. Zach, you keep an eye out for magical traps. Maria, you might be able to help with that too. I'm going first and I'm interfacing with the mercs." His tone brooked no argument, even if he was whispering so low that the shifters behind the bushes couldn't hear him.

Maria and Zach nodded, though Zach looked as if he wanted to argue. Still, he followed the acknowledged Alpha like a good cub and Jesse figured he'd be okay until he saw his parents. At that point, Jesse wouldn't be able to hold the kid back if he really wanted to follow his impulses. And Jesse wouldn't blame him. Not one little bit.

Jesse surveyed the area before stepping out into the small open space between the forest and the shrubs. He'd left Maria and the boy behind a large oak, out of sight. He'd give them a signal after he talked to the jackal.

Sure enough, the shifter was waiting for him behind the opening in the hedges, a smile on his face.

"You got my message," he said.

"I did," Jesse agreed, cradling his weapon casually against his chest. "I wish I could say it was good to see you, Seth."

"Same here, Jesse."

They were wasting precious time, but Jesse had to gauge Seth's stance before he committed any further.

"How'd you get mixed up with *Venifucus*?" Jesse asked point blank.

Seth's expression almost betrayed him, his eyes narrowing and growing cold before he could stop it. That said more than his words to Jesse. Seth still didn't like the *Venifucus*. He hadn't changed all that much from the man Jesse had known in the Middle East.

"It was a commission. Didn't know until we were well into it exactly who had hired us. We're not happy about it. Especially in recent days. We don't kill women and children." Seth spat to the side, marking his words and his territory.

"In that case, will you give us safe passage?"

"Us, who?" Seth looked around in an obvious manner.

"A woman. A boy. Me," Jesse said casually. "My men are on my heels, but we can't wait. The storm is already too intense, and that tells me the bears don't have much time."

"Three then. Safe passage through the maze and a guard at your back in here until your team arrives. When the Wraiths show up, we disappear."

"Agreed." Jesse stuck out his hand and Seth shook it. They had a deal.

"You know," Jesse felt the need to say one thing more. "If you ever get tired of mercing around on your own, you can find me and my men through the Wyoming wolf Pack. For what you'll do this day, you will be welcome among us."

Seth seemed to swallow hard before he could reply, and Jesse was glad he'd offered the olive branch. "Thank you, Alpha. I'll keep the offer in mind."

Jesse gave the signal to Zach and Maria, glad to see Zach take the lead in getting Maria across the ten yards or so of open ground between the woods and the maze. She reached him, relief written plainly in her expression as she slid into the cover of the shrub-enclosed path.

The jackal had slipped away, but Jesse knew he was still around somewhere.

The maze was ornamental in nature, so it wasn't hard to navigate. Many paths led to the center and just as many led out. The path wasn't the hard part. The magical traps were.

They hadn't gone twenty yards yet when Zach's hand gripped Jesse's shoulder. He froze immediately. Maria was a bit behind, but she understood quickly enough and stopped in place next to Jesse. Zach eased around, using hand signals most shifters learned as children playing in the woods. He was able to get his point across. Danger ahead. Magic. Zach was going to recon.

Jesse wanted to argue, but he didn't even feel a tingle. Whatever it was, you had to be more magical than an Alpha wolf to feel it. He turned to Maria.

"Sense anything?" His voice was the barest whisper that wouldn't carry beyond the two of them.

Maria closed her eyes. After a moment, she reached out her fingers to brush the leaves of the nearest hedge. It was some kind of boxwood. The smell of it invaded his nose, but that was normal for this variety of shrub. Even humans could smell boxwoods. The only thing abnormal about these bushes that Jesse could see was their size. They were very old, very tall and clipped back at regular intervals to train them into the shape of the path the gardeners wanted to keep.

"Disturbances. Subtle. Bad feeling. Foul," she whispered, her eyes still shut. "Evil stone. Manmade. Not natural. Blasphemy."

Jesse's eyebrows rose at her words. It sounded like she was channeling the bushes or something, and he wondered if she realized what she was doing. She blinked, coming back to herself and looked at him.

"There appear to be concrete statues placed at intervals along the maze. They are magic. Somehow blood and...other things, were mixed in the concrete, then poured into gargoyle shapes. I think they can animate."

A yelp from just around the corner made Jesse move fast. He turned the corner to find Zach being pinned down by a stone gargoyle twice his size. Damn.

The boy was shifting shape even as Jesse started forward. He pulled the stone giant off the kid who was now much larger and more powerful in his bear form. Bullets wouldn't do any good against concrete, so Jesse tried walloping the thing. If he could break board with his bare hands, he could at least put a dent in concrete.

Sure enough, a fracture showed at the arm joint and it crumbled, falling to the ground. Seeing his success, Zach piled on, pummeling the creature until it was nothing but dust and a little bit of rebar at their feet. It took only minutes, but Jesse knew he was going to be sore the next day. Beating on concrete wasn't easy work.

What he needed was some sort of tool. The rebar caught his eye and he picked up a few pieces, letting the bear sniff them first in case there was some kind of magical residue. Zach shook his head in the negative and Jesse handed Maria two arm-length pieces of metal, arming himself with two more. The kid would stay in bear form for now. He was better off with his claws if it came to more fighting.

And it would. Jesse was fairly certain of that.

Swinging the rebar, they fought their way through two more creatures, much like the first. Jesse sniffed one big cat along their path, but true to Seth's word, his men didn't impede their progress. They didn't help either, but they didn't interfere, which was enough for Jesse at the moment.

They were near the center of the maze now and two of the creatures waited for them around the next bend. Jesse went out swinging, but one of the things had wings. It was going to fly away and raise the alarm, but suddenly it was grounded by...vines. Thick, fast-growing, green vines with big white flowers blooming at intervals as he watched.

Jesse spared a glance for Maria, seeing her crouched to the ground, her hands in the dirt, her eyes on the winged thing that was now tightly held in a net of thick vines. It looked like the dryad part of her was coming to the fore. She was following her instincts as danger came upon them and he couldn't be prouder of her.

"The flowers are a nice touch," he joked as the other

creature fell to dust at his feet with one final blow. He'd hit it so hard, the rebar was bent.

Crude but effective, he was able to dispatch the things much faster using the rebar like a baseball bat or a broadsword, swiping off the heads of the hideous cement creatures with one stroke, then finishing them off with a few more well-aimed blows.

They had a rhythm going. Zach would sniff out the creatures, Jesse would smash them and Maria and Zach pummeled anything that Jesse missed. Little bits of the concrete would continue to wriggle until it was completely smashed and they were helping get those small pieces, so that none of this evil magic escaped.

Chapter Ten

"With all the noise we're making, don't you think they know we're here?" Maria wondered aloud. They'd smashed their way to the center of the maze and were starting to make their way through to the other side and their objective—the pavilion.

"They probably know something is going on, but they're counting on their hired mercs and these...unpleasant statues to handle it," Jesse said quietly, still on the move.

He paused just enough in his description to make her think he'd intended to use a very different word to describe the statues but had censored himself at the last minute. She didn't blame him for what he was thinking. These effing statues were freaking her out, though she didn't dare mention it in front of the men.

She was so impressed by Jesse and Zach. They were working as a team, as if they'd done this a hundred times before. She wondered idly if all shifters were born with the same skills and knowledge of how to work together.

She'd also followed her instincts and found some unexpected skills of her own. Making the flower vines grow had been sheer luck at first. It was something she had never done before, but now that she knew she could coax plants into doing her bidding, she'd be sure to keep that weapon at the ready. There were plenty of growing things in the maze that didn't like the people who clipped, pruned and cut at them all the time. They responded well to her though. They seemed to welcome her influence.

The hedges were old. Old enough to have built up a seething resentment of the way they were constantly cut back and allowed only to grow in the directions the humans wanted. The hedges didn't like the evil statues either. She could use that to their advantage.

The men moved silently ahead of her, leaving the center of the maze and heading for the side of the maze closest to the pavilion. She expected things to get harder from here. As if animated concrete monsters wasn't enough of a problem already.

Another winged gargoyle was just poised to fly when she rounded the corner of shrubbery behind Jesse and Zach. Crouching low, she touched the ground, reaching out to the vines, but there weren't any close enough to the gargoyle. In a panic, she redoubled her efforts, calling on the boxwood hedge behind the creature's pedestal for help.

What she got was more than she ever expected. The hedge all around the grouping of three statues exploded outward in a burst of growth. Zach and Jesse had just begun to engage the two ground-based gargoyles while the middle one on the pedestal was probably set to fly, raising the alarm. The boxwood tendrils wrapped around the raised arms of the fighting gargoyles before they could even strike at Jesse or Zach. And the winged one's limbs and wings were caught in looping branches that grew thicker and more powerful with each second.

The boxwoods really didn't like those statues. Within thirty seconds, all three evil gargoyles had been pulverized by the squeezing, suffocating branches. Both Zach and Jesse turned to look at her with varying degrees of pride and amazement in their expressions.

"Nicely done," Jesse whispered quietly as she straightened and joined them.

She looked at movement just past his shoulder and gasped. For the first time, she saw one of the mercenary shifters. Jesse followed the direction of her gaze and seemed to gauge the situation before nodding once, warily, at the man who stood about fifteen feet away, a gleaming black rifle casually draped across his body. He wore it much the way Jesse did. As if it were an old friend. A companion he was seldom without.

Zach, in bear form, moved toward the man who stood to one side of the path first. When the man made no move to stop him, Zach walked past him and stopped, waiting for Jesse and Maria to join him. Zach was playing the role of point man and doing it rather well, she noted.

Jesse escorted her past the mercenary whose golden hair gleamed in the rays of the setting sun. The eye of the storm was eerily calm with little sound other than their breathing and the occasional rustle of the boxwoods.

"Major Moore?" The merc spoke very softly as Jesse drew even with the man. Jesse kept himself between Maria and the merc at all times.

"And you are?" Jesse replied just as quietly. Nobody would hear beyond two feet away.

"Paxton. Arizona Jaguar Clan. U.S. Navy SEAL, Retired." Maria half-expected him to give his serial number next. "Reports are that whatever your lady just did, it took out all the remaining statues. Only the occasional pedestal is left and a lot of rubble and overgrown bushes." The man cracked a smile and looked around Jesse's bulk to meet her eyes. "Nice going, ma'am." He leaned back just as quickly to talk to Jesse again. "The jackal says he's sorry about the statues. He didn't know. None of us did."

Jesse nodded. "Understood. Tell him thanks."

The man nodded, and as she leaned over to look at him, Maria could just make out the tiny transmitter in his ear and small microphone along his jaw. No doubt all the mercs were connected, keeping tabs on what happened on their patch. She really hoped the mercenaries weren't going to double-cross Jesse and rat them out to the folks who'd paid them to guard this maze. It would be so easy to do with those little radios. One stray transmission and there could be an armored battalion waiting for them at the end of this journey through the shrubs.

"I will. And, sir?" The man had an earnest look in his weary eyes. Jesse remained attentive so the soldier continued. "The jackal told us about your offer. I'd like to look you up after this op is over, if that's all right. It's time for me to find a home."

"If we make it through this, look me up in Wyoming. If I don't make it, talk to my brother, Jason. He'll put you in touch with my men. It'll be up to them, but we don't turn many away."

Jason held out his hand and the man shook it, an expression of relief on his handsome, slightly scarred face. His was a face that had seen a lot and experienced more. Maria's heart went out to him, as it often did to her wounded patients. The animals' wounds were on the outside where she could see them and treat them. This man looked like his wounds were on the inside. Those were probably much harder to heal but just as important.

Once again, Maria was proud of the man she'd fallen in love with so incredibly fast. But who wouldn't love Jesse Moore? He was such a good man. A strong man who led strong men. He'd earned their respect through his actions and deeds. He was a man of honor, and that single facet of his personality touched every part of his life.

Honor was something she valued as well. On a very basic level, they were well matched. The Lady really did know what She was doing when She'd brought them together.

They left Paxton standing to one side of the hedges and moved on. When she looked back a moment later, the jaguar was gone. These shifters were amazingly stealthy.

They rounded another turn in the maze and, as advertised, only an empty pedestal remained. The statue that had been on it was already crumbled to dust beneath a portion of overgrown boxwood hedge. The small tendrils on the ends of the branches reached out to Maria as they passed.

Jesse pulled her back away from the greenery as she gasped at the contact, but she wasn't in danger.

"Sorry. The bushes are...um...grateful, I think. They really didn't like the statues." That was an understatement judging by the silent impressions that boxwood had left with her. "The bushes were just confirming that the path ahead is clear and thanking me for giving them the power to do what they wanted to do all along." She marveled at the idea of communicating with a shrub. She'd never known such a thing was possible.

"You really pack a wallop when you're motivated." Jesse chuckled as he toed through the remains of what had been a statue and then looked up at her with admiration in his gaze.

"I was just following my instincts. You said to do that," she replied almost defensively. "Honestly, I didn't know I could do any of this."

He faced her, his expression full of confidence. "Your instincts probably just saved us a lot of time and hassle. Let's keep going." He looked at the young bear still slightly in front of them. "Zach, you're still on point, just in case there's something else in here we haven't encountered yet."

Maria could clearly see the tent-like slope of the pavilion's white roof over the tops of the tall hedges. They were getting very close now.

They moved through the rest of the maze without further incident. All the statues they passed had been reduced to piles of rubble and Maria felt again the satisfaction of the old boxwoods as she passed each one. A few of the bolder, more powerful bushes reached out leafy stems to her as she passed and their silent communication didn't startle her now that she knew what to expect.

Jesse had kept telling everyone she was descended from some kind of forest dryad. After what she'd been doing the past day and especially here in the maze, she had to believe it now. She'd always thought her affinity for living in the woods was due to the creatures that lived there. She would have to rethink that. Maybe her comfort had really come from the trees and greenery all along, rather than the furry folk.

But those thoughts would wait for another time as they reached the edge of the maze. Jesse moved forward, telling her and Zach with a single look to hang back behind the last of the giant hedges. Maria pressed herself against the lushly growing boxwood, holding her hands out behind her at her sides, palms connecting with the leaves that stirred slightly at her touch.

She motioned to Jesse before he stuck his nose around the edge of the bushes. He came close enough for her to whisper in his ear.

"There are guards facing outward toward the maze at every pillar along the edge of the pavilion," she said urgently. "There's one just on the other side of this hedge. He's got a handgun tucked into his waistband."

Jesse looked upward, where he could probably just see the tops of the pillars over the tops of the hedges. Luckily, they were spaced reasonably far apart and on a disappearing, convex curve. While the guards could probably see each other if they leaned outward from their positions, it might still be possible to take one out without the others noticing. Or so the boxwoods led her to believe.

"I can probably coax a little plant growth to obscure the view of the guys on either side," she offered.

Jesse looked back at her sharply, clearly considering her offer. Finally, he seemed to make a decision.

"Nothing too obvious or they'll come looking. I hesitate to use magic of any kind around this place, but they didn't seem to be prepared for your particular brand of magic. Do it. And if you can trip up the dude I'm going to take out, so much the better."

She smiled at him. "You knock him out. I'll tie him up. There's a friendly clematis trained to grow up the side of each pillar. I can have it attach him to the inside of the pillar where nobody will see him unless they come looking."

"Perfect." He leaned in to place a smacking kiss on her lips before moving to the edge of the bushes once more.

He moved slowly at first. She watched him stalk his prey, scoping out as much as he could of the position of his target while she urged the boxwoods, grass and flowers to grow a bit, obscuring the view of the two men at the pillars on either side. She did her best to make it look natural, not asking any one plant to grow too much. She hoped.

When Jesse struck it was almost too fast for her to see. One minute he was there on this side of the hedges with her and the young bear. The next, he was gone, leaping in an instant to pounce on his prey.

Maria's connection with the boxwood told her what was going on just on the other side of the wide hedge. Jesse clobbered the guard, knocking him out with one quick blow to the temple. It was neat, efficient and barely made a sound.

Jesse propped the unconscious man against the inside of the pillar and Maria knew what to do. She sent a little suggestion through the ground where all things were connected by their roots, to the clematis vine that was struggling to survive in a spot with too little sunlight.

It's positioning didn't matter to Maria. She infused it with the energy of the earth and of her own newfound inner power. The vine sprang to life, twining around the unconscious man with vicious strength. Multiple shoots from the bottom of the plant formed new vines that, while thin, held an unnatural, magical strength.

As a last finishing touch, she let the flowers bloom as Jesse stepped away. The grey-suited man faded into near obscurity, bound by flourishing green leaves to a gray pillar, his unmoving body was festooned with showy white flowers.

Maria smiled as she pulled her power back, thanking the

plant and the earth for answering her call. This sort of thing was beginning to feel natural to her. Who'd have thought she'd be communing so easily with plants even just two days ago?

Jesse returned a few minutes later, a bulky ball of fabric in his arms. He pulled the fabric apart and Maria could see it was three dark robes. Long, black with deep-hooded cowls. Small, medium and large, judging by the lengths of each. Jesse kept the longest one and shoved the medium at Zach, still in bear form, and the short one at her.

"There's a crowd inside. They're all wearing these. Zach, shift and put it on. We need to get to the center of the pavilion and this is the best way I can see to do it." Jesse was tugging the robe on as he spoke.

His main weapon had been moved from slung around his back to resting comfortably right in front of him. The robes opened down the front, so he'd have easy access to the assault rifle should he need it. He looked up at the sky, seeming to search for something. It was still eerily quiet in the eye of the storm, but it had gotten appreciably darker.

"The sun is going down fast now. Less chance of being seen. The only light around the edges of the pavilion where the crowd is gathered is from torches. They saved the spotlights for the center." Jesse looked grim as he said it. No doubt he'd seen what those bastards were doing at the center of the building.

"My parents?" Zach asked, now in human form and covered from head to toe by the robe.

"They're there. Alive from what I could see." Jesse nodded with a grim expression on his face. Zach started forward, but Jesse grabbed his shoulders. "We need to do this calmly. With a plan. Don't let the animal take over. We're going to save them. We're almost there."

Zach gulped and swallowed hard a few times, but he calmed under Jesse's influence. Finally, after a few very tense moments, he met Jesse's gaze.

"I follow you, Alpha." It felt like a ritual vow of loyalty, which impressed the hell out of Maria. She was glad Zach wasn't going to go charging off and get himself killed or captured. At least for now. Who knew how the boy would react when he saw his parents?

Hopefully, by then she and Jesse would be in a position to do something about those evil people in the pavilion. But they had to get in there first.

"All right." Jesse checked them over to see how they looked in the hooded robes. "Let's go. Follow my lead."

They walked in past the unconscious guard roped to the pillar by vines, and nobody seemed to notice. The round pavilion was full of people, all wearing these spooky black robes with the hoods up over their heads. They were chanting and moving their feet in unison as they stood in place, row upon row of them standing in pews that had a permanent look to them. As if this pavilion was used for theatrical or religious events. They were near an aisle that led down to the center. There were six aisles that led from top to bottom and just as many that led only halfway down in the middle of the wedges of seats. Probably to make it easier to get to the seats in the middle as the rows lengthened.

But nobody was sitting. They all stood, chanting words she couldn't understand in an ominously low tone, their feet shuffling as their bodies swayed slightly in place, in unison. Maria's skin crawled. The creepyness factor was off the charts.

They walked in time with the chanting, probably to avoid drawing attention to themselves for as long as possible. Jesse was in the lead. Maria was behind him with Zach bringing up the rear. Their progress was painfully slow, but it made sense to be careful and hang back in the shadows as long as they could.

The area in the center of the pavilion was lit brightly. As they drew closer, she could just make out two figures slumped over in chairs near the center of what looked like a massive fire pit. There was a fire in it, but only a small one off to one side.

At the very center stood a woman in a red robe. The hood on her robe draped down her back and her aristocratic cheekbones and petite frame were surrounded by crackling power. She had one hand stretched out to her side, pointing directly at the two slumped, seated figures. Her other hand stretched skyward, toward the big round hole in the center of the roof. It looked like she was the one using the bears' magic to power the storm.

The woman's icy-blonde hair shone in the spotlights trained on her as night descended more fully. It was almost completely dark now, though the center of the storm was still eerily quiet and lit with the red glow of the last embers of a dying sun. The way they had lit the scene made the woman take on an unearthly aspect. Her body was outlined in pulsing white from the spotlights—*or it could actually be magic.*

The closer they got to the center, the more she could make out. It was hard to see past Jesse's broad shoulders, but she managed to get a glimpse every now and again. She hoped Zach didn't realize his parents were nearly unconscious and bound to the chairs with shiny silver chains.

She didn't like silver. A guy she was dating had given her a silver bracelet for Christmas once and it turned her skin black. Since then, she never went near the stuff, though she had no problem with gold, oddly enough. As long as it was fourteen karat or above.

Her family always gave her gold if they gave her jewelry. She wondered now if her parents were aware that silver was poison to magical creatures like weres and dryads? It didn't seem to affect the humans at the center of the ring, but it certainly seemed able to keep two full-grown grizzlies from breaking the laughably thin chains and walking away.

Suddenly, someone stepped directly into Jesse's path, challenging him. Jesse didn't even try to pretend they belonged there. The man was standing so close that Jesse could only use his fists to drop the guy. Of course, as quiet and efficient as

Jesse did it, the commotion still drew attention. Within moments, they were surrounded.

She heard growling behind her and realized Zach had shifted form again and was scrambling through the crowd in the aisle, slashing as he went. He was making for the center of the pavilion, only a few yards away now. He'd seen his parents and was going for them.

Maria put her back to Jesse, fighting as best she could. The robe had to go. She shrugged it off even as someone grabbed her sleeve. She let him take it, twirling out of the robe and knocking her attacker on his ass in a tangle of fabric at her feet. That kept the rest of them off her for a precious few moments.

Long enough for a shot to ring out. Jesse had a handgun in his left hand and had shot the woman in the center of the pavilion, breaking her concentration. Blood flowed down her arm as she clutched her shoulder. The chanting ceased and pandemonium broke out all over the pavilion as some people began to run for the exits. Others ran to intercept the young bear who was clawing at the silver chains, working to free his parents.

The only reason more people didn't try to get to where Jesse and Maria fought back-to-back was the narrowness of the aisle they were in. They could hold here for some time, but it wouldn't get them any closer to the center of the action and the bear family who needed their help.

At the very moment the thought crossed Maria's mind, a shudder went through the pavilion and a gray mist entered through the hole in the roof and swirled around too fast for the eye to follow. Maria felt the change in the air as an icy cold swooped down from above, smothering all the open flames in the pavilion. All the torches around the perimeter went out in one whoosh. The small cauldron on one side of the enormous fire pit was extinguished as well.

A moment later, bodies started flying from the center of the pavilion out into the crowd. More chaos erupted as more of the acolytes lost their nerve and turned to flee. Jesse pressed forward, down the aisle slowly, working his way through those who remained to block him. Maria fought at his back, though she faced a lot less trouble on the far side of the real action than Jesse did.

He didn't use his gun again, though she thought he would have been well justified to kill anyone who had added their voice to that sickly chant. Still, he was showing restraint and it impressed her on the calmer level of her consciousness.

Finally, they broke through to the bottom of the aisle and the center of the action. There were far fewer people left in their path. Most were running from the combination of bear claws and whatever it was that was launching bloody bodies into the seats in all directions.

Maria finally got a good look and realized the vampire had arrived. Marco was flinging bodies left and right with reckless abandon and superhuman strength. He seemed to be wading through the VIP section of seats off to one side within the fire pit, trying to get to someone in particular. The man in the suit from the woods behind the motel. She saw his face in the chaos before someone else got in her way. That's who Marco was going after.

A quick glance told her Zach was standing in front of his parents, guarding them with equal fervor. Anyone who got within swiping range wound up with bloody furrows in their skin.

It was all very confusing from Maria's point of view, and it got even more so when a new roar echoed through the pavilion, bouncing off the cement pillars and hard surfaces of the curved roof. She looked for the source and wasn't too surprised to see a massive, full-grown grizzly bear wading through the aisle she and Jesse had just left. It was still filled with people trying to get out that were easily swatted aside as the bear forged a bloody path for itself.

No doubt, this was Zach's uncle, Rocky. He didn't even

pause when he reached Jesse and Maria, but charged straight past to where Zach stood trying to defend his weak parents. Rocky took care of anyone still willing to go up against a juvenile grizzly with killing swipes of claws and teeth. Rocky wasn't playing nice. When he used those massive claws of his, he meant business.

Jesse grabbed her hand during a lull and made for the center of the pavilion. The blond woman was still there, sobbing and screaming orders, but few of her followers were still listening to her. When Jesse, Marco and even Rocky tried to get close to her, some kind of magical force kept them away. She had a shield, for lack of a better word, that they could not penetrate.

Maria had an idea and crouched down, touching the cement floor of the old structure. This cement was just sand and rock. No foul magic had been included in its manufacture, and it was old with many cracks that let her reach the earth beneath. She wondered...

Yes. There it was. Just what she needed.

Maria let her power flow downward through the cracks and into the earth, coaxing a deep root she found just where she needed it most. The pavilion began to rumble beneath their feet as the root moved through a crack in the foundation at the center of the fire pit. It rose and erupted directly behind the blond woman in the red robe, sprouting tendrils of the new tree just coming into being.

A mighty oak grew from the sapling, its branches imprisoning the blond woman who had no apparent defense against this sort of magic. Maria felt a moment of triumph as she concentrated all her effort on imprisoning the witch who had caused so much misery. The woman screamed obscenities and then harsh, unintelligible words of dark magic that hurt Maria's ears.

With a flicker of thought, she asked a nearby branch to gag the witch, and it complied, happily doing Maria's bidding. The harsh words ended abruptly, their echoes drowned out by the ominous rumble of breaking concrete as the tree rose higher and the trunk took shape and widened into something very substantial.

The oak was claiming this place, taking on the task of cleansing it. Purifying it. Though it would take a great deal of time. Maria heard all this information in a nonverbal way she couldn't actually explain or adequately describe, but she knew it for the truth. The oak would do what it had been created to do. It would stand sentinel while the dark places were cleansed of evil over the generations of man.

When Maria was satisfied the woman was well and truly trapped and the tree as large as she could get it at the moment, she let go of the power and came back to herself. She wasn't surprised to find Jesse standing over her. What did surprise her was the ring of armed men who surrounded her, protecting her.

They had to be some of Jesse's men. More were all around the pavilion, mopping up the chaotic scene. Prisoners were being secured. Wounded were being segregated for eventual medical attention.

Which reminded her...

"How are Zach's parents?" She stood, addressing Jesse in a rough, weary voice.

He grabbed her arm when she swayed on her feet, dismissing his men to other duties now that Maria was out of danger. Jesse hugged her quickly and then drew her over to where the bears stood vigil over the man and woman still chained to the chairs.

"Silver is poison to many magical races. Marco can't help and even we can't handle it for long periods of time. We're taking turns trying to break the links."

"Hold on." Maria had an idea. Sending a mental request to the nearby tree, she asked it a favor and it complied.

Two branches swayed near enough to work their way into

the links. Maria moved to touch the little branches and give them her power. They quickly grew wide enough to pop the links from the inside. She used a piece of torn fabric she found on the floor to shield her hand as she unwrapped the chains holding the adult bear couple in place. They had awful burns on their skin where the chains had held them and Maria felt more than just silver in the links. The chains had been enchanted, but with the witch held prisoner the spell had been weakened enough to break at the touch of Maria's magic.

She stepped back as the couple were freed. Some of Jesse's men had first aid supplies and appeared to have medical training suited to emergency medicine. Maria was a vet. She didn't deal well with human patients, but would have tried to help if there wasn't anyone else equipped to do so.

"Good job, sweetheart," Jesse complimented her as she moved back. Using so much magic had drained her, but the result was worth every effort. They'd freed Zach's parents and captured some seriously bad people to boot.

"What are you going to do with her?" Maria pointed to the witch being held so efficiently aloft in the tree.

"Good question." Jesse turned to face the vampire who'd stayed well clear of the silver. He had blood all over him and a few dead bodies littered the area where he'd been fighting in the VIP section. "Marco, what are your plans for the mop up? You are the highest authority in these parts. My men stand ready to help and we can transport prisoners back to Wyoming or to the Lords, if you prefer."

"No," Marco said, moving forward with strangely fluid movements. "I have planned this action for many years. The bears' involvement drew you into it and moved up my timetable, but I would have taken action against this group regardless. The owner of this estate is now dead at my hands. I will move in and buy it at the earliest opportunity, then tear it apart, cleansing this area of the evil taint."

Maria swallowed, realizing exactly where some of that blood

on his hands and clothing had come from. She wondered if he'd bitten anyone, but his mouth looked clean. If he had noshed on any of his victims, he was a neat eater.

"I have a dungeon prepared and already the Masters are gathering. We intend to question the witch and her minions until we have learned all we can from them," he went on. "The *Venifucus* threat is real, and this will prove it once and for all to some of my brethren who still doubt." His eyes glowed with anger for a moment before he quelled the show of emotion. "I would, however, welcome assistance in transporting the prisoners to my dungeon. It's not far. I built it especially with these people in mind. I also welcome your Lords or a selection of Alphas to observe the questioning, if you will pass along the message. I am of the opinion that all would-be Guardians of the Light must work together again if we are to thwart Elspeth as we did once before."

"I share your opinion," Jesse said in a grim tone. "My men will deliver the prisoners to your facility at your convenience. I will leave my lieutenant in charge here while I escort the bears to safety. I hope you understand."

At that the vampire cracked a smile. It was a sad smile, but a smile all the same.

"I do understand the need to take them away from this cursed place so they can heal. Go with my blessing. I will work with your junior and look forward to the day our paths cross again."

He held out his hand and Jesse shook it warmly. If she wasn't much mistaken, Maria thought maybe a new friendship had just been forged. At the very least, a new ally had been made. And if evil people really wanted to bring this Elspeth back, Jesse and his folk would need all the allies they could get.

Then the vampire turned to his full attention to her. Maria tried not to gulp.

"Lady, you have begun the work I always intended to do,

bringing forth the guardian oak to dispel the evil of this place. Thank you for sharing your gift so freely. You are indeed a true daughter of the woodland." He took her hand and lifted it to his lips, making her skin tingle in a scary sort of way, though she wasn't really afraid of him. "I once knew one of your talents, many centuries ago. It is clear you are mated to the wolf." Marco's expression turned mischievous and his smile was decidedly inviting. "But if you ever tire of him, I hope you'll look me up."

Was he serious? Maria didn't know how to take his teasing. She'd never been teased by a vampire before. Hell, she'd never even *met* a vampire before.

"Sorry, Master Marco." She wasn't even sure if she was using his title correctly, but she didn't dare call him by his first name alone. It seemed too presumptuous with such an ancient being. "I'm a one-man woman, but thanks for the compliment." She smiled to soften her rejection, but she wanted to be clear. If nothing else, she didn't want Jesse growling at the guy. Not after they'd just formed an alliance. Maria wasn't about to play the Helen of Troy role here.

Thankfully, Marco laughed. "Good to know. Frankly, I always enjoyed baiting werewolves. They're so easy to get a reaction from, but your Alpha is stronger than most. He didn't even growl at me...much." The vampire laughed again and moved away.

Jesse held tight to Maria's hand while he issued orders to his men. Marco himself took possession of the witch when they got her down from the tree. He wasn't taking any chances with her in particular, and he bound her with rune-studded cloths he had secreted in his pockets. Bespelled, no doubt, so that she couldn't use her magic to get away or to cause further harm to anyone.

Jesse's men processed through the prisoners quickly enough. There weren't that many when push came to shove. Many of the outliers had fled early on in the action. The only ones who had stuck around until the end were the diehards. Maria noticed that almost all of them had the tattoos on their wrists and elsewhere. Some even had tattoos on their foreheads.

"You can see those markings, right?" she asked Jesse, remembering his earlier claims about how the tattoos weren't visible to everyone.

"What markings?"

"That guy over there with the bald head, for example. Do you see the band of runes that are tattooed around the perimeter of his head?" She pointed to the man and jumped a bit when he stared directly at her. He knew she was talking about him.

He'd been standing with the other prisoners but moved quickly when Jesse gazed at him thoughtfully and then turned to get one of his men to deal with it. Before Maria knew what was happening, the man with the circle of runes on his head had formed a malevolent yellow fireball in his hands and lobbed it at Jesse's back.

Maria didn't think, she just acted. She held up her hands, palms outward and threw herself in front of Jesse's back, shielding him, though she'd never done such a thing before. The fireball hit her palms and reflected back out, amplified, reacting to anything—or anyone—magical left in the room.

Several of the prisoners dropped where they stood, including the guy with the runes on his head. Maria looked around and realized that everyone who'd fallen unconscious had a mark on his forehead of one kind or another. She tried to tell Jesse as he hugged her close to him in reaction.

He'd been pretty good all night about letting her do her thing, but he'd turned around in the nick of time to see the fireball coming for them, and judging by his reaction, it had worried him.

"You took ten years off my life just then, Maria. Don't do

that again!" He shook her once, but not hard, and then hugged her again. "Wolves are resilient. I can take a hit of magic and the majority of it will bounce off. Most of the time," he added grudgingly. "How did you deflect that much power?"

"I don't know. Still running on instinct here," she reminded him, pushing back away from him, needing some space to breathe. "But I'm glad I did it now, considering the results. All the ones who fell are tattooed on their heads. And did you notice that none of our people were affected? Only the bad guys."

She smiled brightly at him, trying to make him see the good points of what she'd done instead of the danger that had him so worked up. He rolled his shoulders once, as if trying to get rid of muscle tension, and started barking orders to his men. Two heavily armed soldier-types rushed over.

"This is Maria," he explained succinctly. "She is my mate. Her life is more important to me than any other." Maria tried her best not to blush at his statement or the way his men looked at her, but she was sure she failed. "She sees the *Venifucus* markings. I want you to go with her and examine each of the fallen prisoners. One of you will write down her observations and keep good notes on each prisoner who has the markings while the other stands guard. No harm is to come to her, or it will mean your lives. Do you understand?"

Maria thought that last bit was a little harsh, but she didn't dare interfere with the way Jesse ran his group. He was the Alpha here, not her.

Jesse hugged her again and gave her some instructions as well. He really seemed to like giving orders, which was fine with her in this situation, but they'd probably butt heads a bit when the situation wasn't so dire. She looked forward to it.

"Go with them, but stay alert," he counseled. "There could still be danger here. Tell them what you see in as much detail as you can manage. Draw pictures if you can. Every little bit of information we can get on these people could help our cause."

"I understand," she replied just as seriously. If she really was the only one who could see the marks, she had better record them as faithfully as possible for those who couldn't.

"Work fast. I'm going to help the bears and arrange transport. I want to get them to Wyoming as soon as possible."

Chapter Eleven

In the end, it didn't take too long to catalog all the markings each of the prisoners were adorned with. Jesse arranged escort vehicles for the trip back to Pack territory. Rocky insisted on driving Zach and his parents in his own large luxury SUV. Jesse and Maria would be in front of them with escort vehicles loaded with his men, front and back. A little convoy of four vehicles to drive through the night and get them back to the safest place he knew.

They got underway in the wee small hours of the night and made good time traveling steadily west. The storm was beginning to dissipate and move off to the east. Some of the cities along the east coast would get clobbered by rain, but eventually the magically induced storm would blow itself out naturally. Thank goodness.

They drove out of the worst of the residual rain bands by daybreak and started to make even better time. The winds continued to gust at high rates of speed, so flying was still not an option. By the time the storm conditions lessened to where they'd be able to travel normally again, they'd be almost to their destination, so the decision was made to continue over land.

Maria was exhausted by the ordeal of using so much magic in ways she'd never done before. She also hadn't slept in quite a while, so when she started to yawn, Jesse scooted the seat back a little more and encouraged her to lie down, using him as a pillow if she wanted.

Jesse reflected on the outcome of events. They'd done well in rescuing the bears, though both of Zach's parents seemed traumatized by their ordeal. They'd need a lot of time to heal, but Zach was a good kid and he'd protect them—as would Rocky and the Lords. They would spend a little time as guests of Jason and their Pack, but they'd be moving on to the north and Rocky's territory as soon as was practical.

For one thing, the priestesses were there and might be able to do something to heal them of their magical and spiritual wounds. And the Lords had to know everything they could tell them about their abductors and what had been done to them.

That process was going to be emotionally painful for them, Jesse had no doubt. He was glad in a way that he didn't have to be part of that. Better the bears talk to Rocky and the Lords— the former a member of their family and the latter the highest authority over all shifters in this land. They loved Rocky and they respected the Lords. Both would help them through the trauma in ways others simply could not.

Then there was the matter of the prisoners Marco had kept. Jesse wasn't altogether comfortable with the idea of handing over such valuable intel opportunities to the vampire, but the situation had political overtones he preferred not to entangle himself in. Better to leave that stuff to his brother. Jay was better suited to that kind of thing. Jesse was better at fighting and ordering soldiers around. Jason was the negotiator. He would do what was best for the Pack in any political situation. Let him deal with the vampire on the subject of the prisoners.

All Jesse wanted for the next few weeks was his mate and his bed.

They stopped a few times for gas, food and to use rest rooms, but Jesse and Rocky both wanted to get to Pack lands as quickly as possible. The bear family stayed in the SUV for the most part, only getting out to stretch and use the facilities. The glimpses Jesse got of Zach's parents told him they were weak but recovering. They could both walk and tend to their own bodily functions, which was good.

Rocky told him during one of their breaks that they'd been sleeping for most of the journey. Both of them were exhausted. Zach sat vigil from the front seat while his parents slept in the back.

Rocky had even put down the seats at one stop to create a much larger bed area, combining the back seats with the extra-large cargo compartment. He had a sleeping bag and a couple of pillows with him, which they used as bedding. From that point on, the bear couple slept even more comfortably the rest of the way to Wyoming.

When Jesse mentioned this to Maria, he was relieved to hear her opinion that sleep was probably best for the couple after the ordeal they'd been through. Sleep, she assured him, was nature's healer and would help restore the energy that witch had stolen from them.

They drove all day, trading off driving duties occasionally. Rocky allowed one of Jesse's men to drive his SUV while he caught some sleep in the passenger seat. Zach opted to ride with Jesse and Maria during those hours, keeping the car behind them in his sight most of the way. It was a tense convoy, trying to cover ground as quickly as possible and being extra vigilant should their enemies try something.

The grizzlies were vulnerable while their energy was so low. They were being guarded as closely as possible, but they wouldn't be truly safe until they were behind the protections of Pack land. At least not to Jesse's mind. He'd tried to explain it to Maria, but he wasn't sure she really understood his feelings on the subject.

Jesse had fought in a half dozen foreign lands, and those experiences had given him a new appreciation for the mountaintop and surroundings he called home. In all his travels, he'd never found a place he felt safer or more secure. It wasn't just the place. It was the people too. His family, his friends, his men. All combined, it spelled home and it was the safest place he knew.

That protection would extend to their guests. Rocky and his family would be made to feel just as welcome and just as protected. Once the Pack extended its hospitality, they would fight to the last wolf, tooth and claw, to protect their invited guests.

They stopped again around dinner time, and Zach went back to Rocky's SUV. They got food to go and ate on the road, not wanting to stop too long. They were safer on the move should anyone be after them. And after the ruckus they'd caused in that pavilion, Jesse was pretty sure someone would be after retribution.

If they moved quickly enough, the pursuit would never catch up to them.

When Maria started yawning again soon after dinner, Jesse scooted back the seat again and invited her to sleep. She started out resting her head against his shoulder, but sometime during the long drive her head wound up in his lap.

They were much closer to Pack lands—perhaps an hour away—when Maria woke up and seemed to realize where she was resting her cheek. And what her presence in his lap had done to him over the past half hour or so. Jesse was hard as a rock.

Maria had no idea how she'd ended up with her cheek pressed up against a ridge of hard flesh covered by only a couple of thin layers of fabric. The last thing she remembered, she'd been leaning against Jesse's shoulder... Although there was some vague recollection of sliding into a more stretched-out position at one point.

Damn. She'd slept herself right under the steering wheel—which he must've adjusted upward somehow—and into his lap. All in all, it wasn't a bad place to be. She was as comfortable as she could be sleeping in such a cramped space, and she liked the scent of him. The faint trace of gun oil and cordite only added to the danger of his allure.

She had it bad. There was no doubt. She'd missed him in the hours since they'd last made love. If that was what you'd call being banged up against a tree. She wouldn't have believed it only a few days ago, but something sacred and special had happened at that rest stop in that leafy circle of trees.

Her soul had joined to his, never to be parted. And part of that joining was the shared need they had for each other. His was evident—pressing up against her cheek, seeking her touch. Hers was ever present and always ready. She wanted him, no matter what the circumstances.

While she'd bet he was probably going to be the dominant partner in this relationship when it came to sexual matters, she knew in this situation she definitely had the upper hand. *Wouldn't it be fun,* she thought with an exceedingly naughty impulse, *to give him a ride he'd always remember?*

They hadn't been able to fuck each other's brains out for hours and hours while they helped Zach and his family. They were alone now and on their way to somewhere they'd most likely have to answer a lot of questions before they could sneak off and be on their own. Jesse probably needed her as much as she needed him, and she could give him this little gift so easily.

As long as he didn't run them off the road.

She thought about it for a split second and then realized she trusted him to keep them safe even while she blew his mind...and other parts of him. With a wicked grin, she turned her head and lifted one hand to his fly.

"What are you doing, babe?" Jesse sounded a little nervous and her smile widened.

"You mean you don't know?" She couldn't resist teasing him.

"Uh..." He cleared his throat as she released his cock from the confines of his pants. Poor baby had probably been hard for a while, judging by the state of him as he strained against her fingers.

"You just keep your eyes on the road and hands on the wheel. Let me take care of the rest." Even to her own ears, her voice sounded kind of sultry. She was amazed by the way Jesse affected her. She'd never even known she had a sex-kitten side before.

She took him into her mouth after a few preliminary strokes with her hand. He was so hard she didn't want to prolong his agony...too much. Licking him like a lollipop, she savored the taste and texture of him, learning him as she'd wanted to since almost the first moment they'd met. Certainly from the first time they'd made love.

She wanted to know everything about him. What made him want. What made him come. What touches he liked best. Everything there was to know about him sexually.

Maria already had a good concept of his character and would get to know more of his thoughts the longer they were together, but the forbidden knowledge of his sexual appetites were on her mind now. She wanted to drive him wild and make him come so hard he'd forget all the other women he had to have known and focus on her alone.

She didn't know much about *were* mating except what she'd heard from Jesse already and what the cougar woman had told her. It was a mixed picture at best. What she wanted was to have Jesse's undivided sexual attention if they were going to make a go of this relationship. She'd already committed to him, but she knew relationships took work to make them thrive. She was willing to put in that work...especially the most pleasurable kind she was doing now.

She felt his excitement rise as she went down on him. The steering wheel was gripped with white-knuckled intensity and she wondered if he could break the thing if he held it too hard. Smiling, she returned to her work, sliding down and up on him repeatedly, using her hands and mouth to create a rhythm that seemed to drive him wild.

Jesse was growling deep in his chest and the sound really turned her on. He let go his death grip on the wheel and slid one hand down her back, over the curve of her buttocks and up under the hem of her shorts. She was kneeling on the length of the bench seat, her ass in the air. She kept low so she wasn't visible through the windshield.

Jesse's talented fingers found her core, and suddenly the stakes of her little game changed dramatically. He slid two thick fingers up her channel as his cock went down her throat. She moaned and felt him shudder as her body responded to the harsh rhythm he set up in her channel.

At that point it became a bit of a race to see who could get the other off first. They both won, coming together as the car rocked and rolled down the highway. Jesse's steering was a little iffy for a few moments as the climax hit, but as she'd known he would, he kept them safely on the road.

She swallowed his salty come as his fingers continued a slow pulse inside her, basking in the afterglow of the hardest, quickest orgasm yet. If he was this good in a pinch, she wondered how she would survive when they finally had the leisure to spend all night in bed together without anywhere to be the next day.

Maria couldn't wait to find out.

When they finally stopped sometime later in front of a beautifully crafted, giant house set in the woods, Maria was relieved. Her whole body vibrated with the rhythm of the wheels and she thought it might take some time before she didn't feel as if she was still moving down the highway at illegal speeds instead of standing still on *terra firma*.

A man who looked a lot like Jesse came out to meet them. On closer inspection, he was a younger version of her guy. Younger both in years and in mileage, judging by his open expression and calm eyes. A tall woman followed him down the steps of the house. Sally.

Maria had seen them both before, of course, on the video link, but they looked slightly different in person. Bigger, for one thing. Jason was as broad shouldered as Jesse and just as tall. His wife was tall for a woman, though she looked downright petite standing next to the oversized men.

Sally came right over to Maria and smiled brightly, offering a tentative hug. It was a little awkward, but Maria was glad to meet her supposed cousin. The more she had done with magic over the past few days, the more she believed there was some truth to the whole dryad story.

"Can you hear it?" Sally asked her as they walked slowly together toward the big house. "The trees are singing. Welcoming you."

"Um..." Maria stretched out her newly honed senses and she felt the welcome, but she didn't hear anything. "I think maybe I perceive things a little differently than you do. Do you actually hear a song?"

Sally looked at her, surprised. "Yeah. I hear the song of the leaves and branches. Don't you?"

"Not really." Maria felt a little defective—and defensive. Her magic wasn't trained. It was all instinct on her part. Sally's expression dropped and Maria felt bad. "I feel the welcome though. The woods are happy."

Sally brightened and Maria was glad she'd made the effort. People were piling out of SUVs and the house, each group helping the other while Rocky's SUV was moved closest to the stairs leading up to the house. Jesse was with his brother, talking to Rocky and helping Zach's family. For the moment, Maria was on her own with Sally.

"What is this place?" Maria asked, standing for a moment to take in the majestic house that fit so beautifully into its environs.

"It's the Pack House," Sally explained, standing beside her.

"It's a communal building where any member of the Pack can seek shelter in times of need, and there's a giant hall attached to the back of it where enormous meals are served three times a day. Werewolves eat a *lot*."

Maria laughed with Sally as they resumed their slow walk to the front door.

"Jason keeps his office here, so when we go home we're really home. The Pack knows not to bother us there unless it's a real emergency." She kept talking as they mounted the wide stairs. "There was a lot of boundary testing when we first got together. The soldiers all recognized me for an Alpha right away, but some of the others in the Pack needed a little more convincing. Of course, with Jason and Jesse's fellas behind me, there was no real question of my status. If you stick around long enough, you'll learn that wolves are really caught up in the hierarchy of the Pack. Especially the women." Sally rolled her eyes as she ushered Maria into a large entryway and then through into a sort of parlor or living room.

"I guess I can understand that. And I suppose you'll be seeing a lot more of me since, uh...Jesse and I are, um, together." Maria sat on a wide couch, weary to her bones after the mad dash cross country.

Sally stopped dead. "Really?" Sally seemed surprised at first and then a big smile broke over her features. "Is it serious? Is he really as gruff as he seems? I love Jason, but honestly, Jesse scares me a little. He's very intense."

Maria had to laugh as she took a seat in an overstuffed chair cattycorner to the couch. "Oh yeah, he is intense, but in a really good way." A little blush heated her cheeks, she knew, but it felt good to talk about her and Jesse's relationship out in the open. There'd been nobody to tell about it until now, with her aunt and grandmother holed up out in the family cabin, incommunicado.

As if speaking about him had conjured him up, Jesse walked in and flopped down on the couch next to Maria, throwing one arm behind her along the back of the couch. He looked tired now that they'd arrived safely at their destination.

"I guess she told you?" Jesse's words were for Sally as he dropped his arm to Maria's shoulders and pulled her in close against his warm side.

"Told me what exactly?" Sally's eyes narrowed although a smile hovered over her lips.

"That I just added another dryad to our Pack." He laughed as he said it and squeezed her tight against him. "Maria is my mate, Sal. We already sealed it inside a sacred circle. It's a done deal."

Sally squealed and jumped out of her seat, leaning in to hug first Maria, then Jesse, then Maria and Jesse together.

Jason walked into the room and Sally jumped up and hugged him too. "Did you know Jesse and my new cousin were an item?" she accused playfully.

"I suspected, based on Jesse's evasiveness every time I mentioned the good doctor, but I wasn't sure." Jason grinned broadly as he came over to the couch. Jesse stood and accepted his brother's back-pounding hug. "Congratulations, Jes," Jason said as he released his older brother. He turned to Maria and took her hand, helping her up from the couch to stand in front of him. "I know you're not well versed in how things work around here, but Sally and I will help in any way we can. Welcome to the Pack, Maria." He hugged her and Maria felt the true feeling behind his words. She was touched by the genuine warmth of Jesse's younger brother and feeling just a tiny bit overwhelmed.

"All right, all right. That's enough of that." Jesse pulled her away from his brother playfully and wrapped one arm around her waist, drawing her close. "You've got your own woman, Jay. This one's mine."

They all laughed at the brotherly ribbing, and although Maria would've loved to talk more with her supposed cousin to try to figure out where she fit in, a jaw-cracking yawn didn't go unnoticed. Jason moved back and Sally seemed sympathetic.

"You've been on the road all day," Jason stated, moving toward the door. "You're probably tired. Are you going up to your place or do you want to crash here for the night?"

Jesse turned to look at Maria and caught her yawning again. "Much as I'd love my own bed right now, I think we'd better get horizontal as soon as possible. We're both pretty tired. I guess we'll use one of the guest rooms here, and I can show Maria our place up the mountain in the daylight so she can get the full effect."

"Good," Jason said decisively. "I already had one of the women fix up the suite on the southwest corner for you." He rubbed his hands together as he led the way out of the parlor. "Don't worry about your vehicle. I've got someone taking care of all the loose ends. Your duffle bags should already be in your rooms and you're just down the hall from the bears, in case you were wondering. I've got extra security on the Pack house tonight and will keep that going until the bears move on, but we can discuss details for their protection tomorrow, Jesse. I'm going to need your help with that."

"Of course." The two men moved forward together back into the main entryway, discussing plans for the morning, leaving the women to follow.

Sally caught Maria's hand and her attention. "I'm really glad to have you here, Maria. Maybe we can find a little time tomorrow to talk."

"I'll look forward to it," Maria said politely, meaning every word. Now that she was here and had met these folks in person, she wanted to learn more about them.

If they really were going to be part of her family, she had a lot to discover and a lot to tell them as well. For one thing, she would bet her last nickel that her aunt and grandmother were already on their way, wanting to know all about Maria's new beau. They'd already foreseen him, but now that the storm was over, they'd want to meet him and his people. And they wouldn't wait for an invitation. Of that she had little doubt.

The Alpha pair left them at the grand staircase and Jesse made her yelp when he snatched her up in his arms and carried her up the stairs like something out of "Gone With the Wind". She was secretly glad. She was so bone weary that she hadn't been looking forward to mounting all those stairs on her own two feet.

Jesse seemed to know exactly where he was going in the big house, so she closed her eyes and nestled her head against his shoulder, willing to let him take her wherever he wanted to go. Though she did open her eyes a few times just to get a glimpse of her surroundings.

Jesse carried her through a couple of hallways and down a corridor marked by closed doorways at more or less regular intervals. Sort of like a hotel but not quite. It wasn't as sterile in its décor for one thing. And the spaces between rooms was much larger. Everything here was built on a grand scale.

He opened a door, jostling her a bit but refusing to put her down. Jesse carried her across the threshold and kicked the door shut behind them. She looked around and realized they were in a sitting room. French doors were open to an inviting bedroom only a few yards away, and as he approached the soft-peach room, she noted another open door to a luxurious bathroom where steam was rising from a bathtub filled with lightly peach-scented water.

"Oh, man, does that look good. Is that bath for me?"

Jesse walked into the bathroom and set her down, finally, on her feet in front of the bathtub.

"Yes, ma'am. A relaxing soak for you. A quick shower for me to wash away the miles and help us both unwind a little so we can rest well tonight." He pulled his T-shirt off over his head. "Hop to it, missus." He flicked her playfully with the shirt before throwing it in a hamper in the corner.

Her tired brain fixated on the hamper. "Do they have laundry service here?"

"Sort of. We're only staying one night, but the ladies on laundry duty will make sure our clothes find their way back to my place after they're laundered. We all help each other in the Pack. I protect. Some of the older ladies seem to like doing domestic tasks. A few of the older gents keep the screen doors from squeaking and fix the appliances, that sort of thing. Everyone pitches in, doing what they're best inclined to do."

"Sounds a little like a commune," she observed, removing her travel clothes. She felt decidedly grungy after so many hours on the road.

Jesse laughed at her comment as he undressed near the lavishly tiled shower in the corner of the big room. "We tend to rely on ourselves more than the outside world, though Jason's made some changes that allow us to mix a little more freely with humans than we did before. Most of our kids attend college now. A generation ago, that was forbidden. We seldom interacted with humans and mixed marriages were discouraged to the point of banishment."

"Wow. That's harsh." She slipped off her underwear and placed all her clothes in the hamper before submerging herself in the fragrant water of the bathtub.

"We've been sort of reexamining history since this thing with the *Venifucus* blew up again. It seems that during the last great battle against Elspeth, all the Other races banded together and worked in unison to bring about her defeat. After that, they went their separate ways. Over the centuries, the alliances broke down and suspicion and fear took over. I tend to think the *Venifucus*—who never really went away, we now realize— were behind a lot of the dissention. I think they fomented anger and distrust between our races and even among humans."

"That's...diabolical." But Maria could see the truth in his

ideas. Somebody had turned werewolves and vampires into super villains even in human society. Growing up, she'd never heard one good thing about either race—although that was starting to change. Maybe Jason's decision to allow the Pack members more interaction with human society was having an influence.

"Yeah, it is. But we're working to change all that. We're forming alliances with Others. Shifters of all kinds, magic users who are on the right side of things, even bloodletters, as you saw." Jesse turned on and adjusted the water in the shower before diving in.

On her side of the bathroom, the warm water was having a relaxing effect on Maria. She began to drift as a very naked Jesse stepped into the shower, out of sight. Damn, he was gorgeous. She wondered again what a man built like that really saw in her? She wasn't going to question it too closely because she didn't want to jinx things, but she felt lucky to have him. Not only was he a man of honor—one of the most important attributes in any person, in her opinion—but he was built like a Greek god. On steroids.

Did the bath water suddenly get hotter? Maria felt flushed and she knew the cause. He was standing under a hot spray of water only a few feet away from her. They were both naked but separate. She really needed to do something about that.

Maria washed off, using a brand new scrubby that still had the tag on it. These guest suites were really stocked well, if this bathroom was any indication. She rinsed her hair using the handheld sprayer and luxuriated in peach-scented heaven while Jesse took a shower so hot that steam billowed out into the room. Or maybe, she thought with a giggle, water just sizzled into steam when it touched him. He was certainly hot enough all by himself.

"What's so funny?" Jesse's voice rumbled near her ear, making her jump. Her eyes popped open and she realized she'd been so caught up in the hypnotic heat of the water combined with her own thoughts that she hadn't even heard the shower cut off. Jesse sat on the rim of her tub, a towel wrapped low around his hips.

Her mouth went dry. Damn. He really was as beautiful as a man could be.

The silence dragged on until his gaze went from amused to molten. He reached over and pulled the plug on the drain.

"Come on. Let's get you out of there. I have a surprise for you."

She didn't say a word as he held out a heated towel for her to step into. He wrapped it around her, taking a moment to give her a hug from behind and nibble on her ear. Goosebumps rose on her arms, and he chuckled, noticing his effect on her.

He guided her out of the giant bathroom, through the bedroom and into the sitting room. A rolling tray with a plethora of covered dishes stood to one side of a small table by the window that was now set with two place settings. Crystal goblets of water and beautiful china graced the table, as did a single red rose in a crystal vase and a candle ready to be lit.

Maria gasped, taking it all in for a moment.

"I thought you might be hungry." Jesse sounded a little uncertain at her back.

She turned and stared up at him. "This is the most romantic thing anyone has ever done for me," she said seriously, smiling to keep from weeping at his thoughtfulness. "Thank you."

His expression went from nervous to confident as he bent to place a chaste kiss on her lips. She wanted more, but he wouldn't allow her to take the kiss deeper. A little annoyed but willing to play the game his way for now, she stepped back and moved toward the table.

Jesse served what had to be the most delicious, exotic, romantic meal of her life. He lit the candle, and though there was no alcohol served, the water was even better. Mountain-spring fresh and filled with a magical sparkle that spoke volumes about the source and the lands from which it came. Pack lands, Jesse told her. There were natural springs all over the mountain from which they drew their water, and they did their duty as custodians of this woodland, to keep the land pure, the way nature intended.

She could tell. The spring water was invigorating in a way that most other water in the human world was not.

Maria didn't realize how hungry she was until the aromas hit her as Jesse lifted the covers off the dishes of food. He ate easily three times the amount that she did, which was fine with her since the helpings were generous. There was even desert, though that was not as huge a portion as the meat had been, which made sense to her. Wolves were carnivores, after all.

She enjoyed the cherry cheesecake, eating every last crumb. After the past few days of travel, fear, fighting and worry, she figured she deserved a little splurge.

As she licked the last creamy bits off her fork, she became aware that Jesse was staring. She looked at him, going from oblivious to very tuned in to him in a flash. Her licking motion on the fork stuttered to a halt and then started again with new purpose. She went slower, teasing him, showing him her tongue and hoping it reminded him of what she could do to him with it.

Judging by the bulge in his towel, they were on the same page.

She kept licking until the very last bit of cheesecake was gone. Jesse watched her every move, his mouth parted slightly until she put the fork down. He sat there for a moment before his eyes narrowed and a low, sexy growl rumbled through his chest.

He stood and scooped her into his arms, quick as a flash, taking her into the bedroom and kicking the doors shut behind him before tossing her onto the lush bed. She bounced a little, laughing at his eagerness. She felt exactly the same. She'd waited too long to have him all to herself, in a bed where they didn't have to rush.

Jesse threw his towel to the floor and reached for hers. Rolling her out of it, he pounced on her the moment she came to rest on her belly. One of his hands was on either side of her face and she could feel his knees brushing against the outsides of her thighs.

He lowered his upper body, rubbing his lightly furred chest against her back and growling. She felt the rumble pass through his chest and into her body. The feel of it—of him—made her breath catch. Damn. That was sexy.

Her head was turned to one side and he brought his face down next to hers, nibbling on the sensitive skin of her neck and licking around the whorls of her ear. He nipped her earlobe, making her shiver.

"I've been dreaming of this, my love." Her breath caught again at his gentle words, spoken in a gruff whisper.

"Me too," she admitted on a low moan that seemed to turn him on even more. She could feel the thick shaft of his cock now, nestling against the soft curves of her ass. She wanted more.

Always, with Jesse, he made her want him so effortlessly. She was so hungry for him she barely needed any foreplay at all. She tried to push back against him, but apparently he had other plans.

Jesse pushed her shoulders down as he rose over her, at the same time lifting her hips with one strong hand on her belly. He positioned her on her knees and then moved downward to part her legs so that her ass was up in the air and her pussy exposed to him in a blatantly sexual way.

Doubt crept in as he remained silent. Maria hadn't been taken doggy style in a long time, but considering she'd just sealed her life to a man who was part wolf, she supposed she'd better get used to it. The thought made her smile.

Her smile turned into a gasp of shock when a long, wet tongue suddenly plunged into her from behind. Jesse shaped her ass with his hands, spreading her wider as his tongue plundered her slick folds. She cried out. She couldn't help herself. No man had ever done her like Jesse was doing her. Frankly, she wasn't sure how much of this amazing treatment she could stand. Already her tummy was shivering with shocks of pleasure, her hips undulating as he brought her to peak after peak, driving her higher with every stroke of his tongue.

"Jesse!" she cried out as he drove her to another hard, fast climax. She shivered in his hold, bucking hard now.

He finally relented, chuckling as he drew away from her pussy. She felt him come over her again, though he kept her on her knees with her ass up. She thought she knew what might be coming next and she could hardly wait. Despite the small quakes of satisfaction he'd already given her, she wanted more. She wanted all of him. Now and forever.

"I like the way you say my name, Maria, my love," he growled sexily near her ear.

He nipped her again as he brought the head of his cock to her folds and slid around in the wetness there, teasing her, tormenting her, holding what she most wanted just out of reach. She tried to push back onto him, but he wouldn't allow her to move.

"Please, Jesse. I need you," she begged. She wasn't above pleading for what she wanted, and he seemed to like it. She felt him pulse against her and his cock slid inside her, just the tip of him, before he stopped.

"Tell me how you feel about me, Maria. I need to hear it."

Now? He was denying her and he wanted her to talk to him *now*? If she could growl like him, she would have. As it was, she turned her head to look up at him, ready to speak her mind when she saw the expression on his face.

He looked...needy. Open. Uncertain. And absolutely

adorable. He'd let down his barriers and wanted her reassurance in a stunning move that made her respect him all that much more.

Her heart melted and she couldn't deny his need.

"I love you, Jesse," she said simply, her voice full of the love in her heart for the man who had made all her dreams of a lover come true.

His eyes showed his relief as his lips smiled in pleasure of the emotional kind. "I love you too, my mate. Don't ever doubt it." He shoved fully inside her, joining them in the way of mated couples.

His strokes were long and languorous at first, escalating over time into hard, fast digs that nearly lifted her knees off the bed. He moved her body around as if she weighed nothing at all, adjusting his hold on her hips and his position in her pussy to suit his whim and to bring her the most amazing pleasure she'd ever known. She came and came for him, crying out his name multiple times before he finally joined her in the spasming bliss that was theirs alone in this vast and beautiful universe.

Chapter Twelve

Jesse woke her early for more leisurely loving. They'd spent the whole night drifting between intense pleasure and blissful sleep. She woke to another round of ecstasy and then joined him in the shower for a playful romp that included a full demonstration of all the creative uses for a loofah.

Maria felt decidedly naughty when they emerged from their suite and went down for breakfast. Jesse led her to the big hall at the back of the house where meals were served. It was set with long tables and chairs and an almost overflowing buffet had been set up along one end of the room. People sat in small groups or pairs at various tables in no seeming order, and the noise level was low since it was still relatively early in the day.

"Most of us get up kind of late compared to humans," Jesse explained as they took plates and began walking down the buffet, taking portions of whatever appealed. "The safest time to run is at night, when humans are in bed and it's dark enough that anyone who is out and about can't really see us."

"That makes sense," Maria commented as she noted the wide selection of different kinds of breakfast meats.

There was even a station where one young wolf was making omelets to order. It wasn't terribly formal. The college-aged kid wasn't in any sort of uniform and he was sitting at a nearby table reading what looked like a chemistry textbook until someone wanted an omelet. Everyone seemed to know everyone else and the atmosphere was friendly. Maria liked the vibe right away.

When they neared the young man studying chemistry in between making what looked like amazingly fluffy, giant omelets, Jesse greeted him with a pat on the back. He spoke a few words in the youngster's ear and the young man immediately jumped up to make whatever Jesse had requested.

Maria already had a plate full with a couple of slices of crisp bacon and French toast dripping with butter and powdered sugar. That was plenty for her, but Jesse's plate was already heaped with meat when he led her to a table near the center of the room. They settled in, using the thermal carafe filled with coffee already on the table to pour two cups for themselves. The young man brought over his completed creation on another plate a few minutes later. From what Maria could see, it was a four-egg omelet with all kinds of vegetables and cheese oozing out from the sides.

"So what do you think?" Jesse seemed eager for her approval and she smiled as she dug into her French toast.

"I think if you guys eat like this every day, I could get really fat here in no time at all." She laughed, and he did too, but in the back of her mind she realized she'd have to moderate her own eating around here. She wasn't a werewolf. She didn't have that super-fast metabolism that allowed them all to eat so much amazingly good food.

"You're perfect, Maria. You will always be perfect to me." His tone was touchingly sincere, as was the look in his eyes when she met his gaze.

"I love you, Jesse," she whispered, reaching out to touch his hand, sharing the special moment with him. Those simple words said everything that was in her heart. All the complicated feelings could be boiled down to that simple, life-altering phrase.

She wasn't sure how long they sat there, gazing goofily into each other's eyes when a throat cleared rather loudly right behind them. She jumped back an inch or two, swiveling her head to look up, and found Zach's Uncle Rocky standing behind them with two plates of food in his hands.

"I've been looking for a moment to speak to you both privately," he said gruffly. "This seemed like an opportune time...unless you want to be alone?" He smiled knowingly at them and Jesse laughed, welcoming the grizzly shifter to sit with them.

"Yeah, I think it's about time you met Doctor Garibaldi," Jason said as if he knew something she didn't.

"Garibaldi." Rocky repeated her surname with significance as he sat down opposite them and placed his plates on the table.

Maria held out her hand politely and Rocky took it in his. When their skin met, she felt a strange tingle of magic. Something familiar, but she couldn't quite place it. Now she was intrigued.

"Maria, you haven't formally met Zach's uncle, Rocco Garibaldi." She could feel Jesse studying her reaction and Rocky's grip tightened a fraction, sending that little zing of familiar magic up her arm.

Maria was confused. "But Zach's last name isn't the same, right?" She couldn't remember if they'd ever discussed her surname or Zach's. It seemed a bit too much of a coincidence that they should all have the same last name.

"Zach is my sister's cub. She married a Collins. He took his father's last name, as did my sister, but she was born a Garibaldi." He finally let go of her hand and she felt the residual tingle. "The question is are we related somehow? It seems odd you would get mixed up with Zach and his troubles if you weren't somehow already joined to us by blood and magic. Is there shifter blood in your background?"

"I don't honestly know. My real dad died when I was young. My mother remarried and my stepdad thinks my aunt and grandmother are crazy old hippies. They're the ones who tried to teach me about magic, but they never mentioned shapeshifters. The first time I ever heard of such a thing was when I treated a cougar brought to me by a rescue organization. She'd been hit by a car, they thought. I performed surgery to fix her up and over time, as she healed and began to trust me, she took a big chance and shifted in front of me. I was shocked. I never thought such a thing was possible. She calmed me down and we became friends. She eventually healed and left my sanctuary. She didn't want to stay too long in one place in case her husband caught up to her. He was the car." She saw the confusion on Jesse's and Rocky's faces and knew she had to explain.

"Sorry." She shook her head. "What they'd thought was damage caused by collision with a car was really the result of a beating. Her husband was abusive and nearly killed her. I listed the cougar as having died of its wounds on all official paperwork and she was free to start her life over. She contacts me every now and again. So far, he hasn't found her and she's living a much better life."

"That was a good deed you did, Doctor," Rocky said in his gruff voice. Maria was uncomfortable with his compliment, so she went on with her explanation.

"I didn't realize Zach was a shifter when he came to me. He'd been shot and I removed the bullet and took care of him like I'd care for any of the animals brought to me. I still feel so bad about locking him in the cage. I've had problems with people trying to steal some of the exotic animals, so I started using locks. I had no clue about Zach until Jesse spotted him. I'm very sorry."

She was afraid of the older grizzly's reaction, so she'd come clean as quickly as possible. She didn't want this standing between them. If he was going to have a problem with her, best to get it out in the open and deal with it right away.

But she needn't have worried. Rocky shrugged off her words and remained calm.

"It's one of the hazards of wearing our fur. You did what you could for him and it was really up to him to let you know he wasn't a regular bear—like your cougar friend did. Zach should have sensed the magic about you and realized you could be trusted from your actions."

"He was pretty out of it most of the time." She found herself defending Zach. "His wounds were extensive."

"Thank you for patching him up and taking care of him. And for everything that came after. You did an amazing job in helping to free my sister and her mate and capture those responsible. Our side won a decisive victory this time, and it's due mostly to your actions, Maria. I'm sure the Lords will want to thank you as well."

Maria felt her cheeks heat with a flush as she smiled. "You're welcome," she replied softly. "It was the least I could do."

"And more than anyone else, my love." Jesse took her hand, holding it on top of the table where everyone could see.

"So it's true then?" Rocky asked with a growing smile. "You've tamed the wild wolf at last." His gaze invited Maria to join in his obvious merriment. "Congratulations to you both."

"Thanks," Maria replied softly while Jesse only grinned.

She was going to say more when Jason and Sally walked over and joined their table with greetings all around. It was a few minutes before they all settled again and Rocky brought the conversation back to the point he'd been asking about before.

"How far back can you trace the Garibaldi name in your ancestry, Maria?" Rocky asked casually as they ate.

"I'm not sure, but Nona—my father's mother—would have those records. She keeps track of the family."

"There's an easier way," Sally piped up from her end of the table. "Leonora showed me how to see my family tree. I bet you could do it too, Maria."

She couldn't quite imagine what Sally was talking about, but she was definitely interested. Jesse had mentioned something about this early on when they'd first met and the idea had taken root in her mind.

"I'm willing to try. If it works it could answer a lot of questions."

Sally smiled brightly. "Okay. After we're finished eating we'll go outside. Our kind of magic is best suited to the woods, so it'll be easier if we're in them."

"That makes sense," Maria agreed and the conversation turned to other things.

Jason talked about his early morning conversation with Marco the vampire and how the Lords were sending representatives to observe and take part in the questioning. Rocky told them how Zach and his parents were being served breakfast in their suite. They were slowly regaining their strength and planned to stay a few days at the Pack house before moving on with Rocky to his home territory.

"Their home was completely compromised," Rocky added with a frown. "Not to mention destroyed by the bastards who abducted them. Apparently, they ripped the place apart looking for anything magical or any information that would lead to more members of their Clan, family and friends. We're all pretty careful not to leave that kind of information lying around, so I don't think they got much, but it's best to be on guard. I've alerted the rest of the family and Clan. There aren't many of us, so it's easily done."

"And the bad guys were mostly captured," Maria thought out loud.

Jason frowned at her. "I'm sorry to say that's no guarantee of safety. The *Venifucus* have a worldwide operation with tentacles everywhere. Whatever information the group in Nebraska stole from the Collins home is no doubt already in the databases and being studied by other members of their organization."

That didn't sound good.

"And there's more, Maria," Sally broke in with a concerned

expression. Maria had seen Sally checking something on her smartphone. "I just heard that the people you asked to watch your animals reported a break-in early this morning when they went over to your place to do the morning feed. The local cops went out to check things. Looks like the perps ransacked your home but left the animals alone for the most part."

Her stomach sank at the news and Maria put her fork down. She couldn't eat another thing. Her appetite was shot.

"Excuse me for a minute." She pushed away from the table and moved out of the room. She heard Jesse following a few steps behind her and she was glad of his presence and the fact that he was giving her a little space but not leaving her alone at this awful moment.

Maria went for the wide doors that led out onto a deck that faced the backyard bordered by dense forest. She removed her cell phone from her pocket. She'd kept it switched off and used it only once the day before during the long drive to check with her friends who'd promised to take care of her sanctuary. Everything had been okay at that time.

Maria hit speed dial and waited impatiently for the call to connect. She stood on the deck in dappled sunlight and her heart wanted to appreciate the beauty all around her, but her mind was caught up in what might be happening back home.

Although...it really wasn't home anymore when she stopped to think about it. Home was standing a few feet behind her. She turned to look at him as the call connected.

As she talked to her friend, she realized something of major importance. The sanctuary she had built really wasn't *her* sanctuary anymore. Her home, her place of safety, her security was tied to Jesse now.

Somehow, knowing that, she calmed and was able to deal with the nuts and bolts of what was going on back in Iowa. Her friend went over the sequence of events as she knew them and Maria pieced together the rest. She reassured her friend that everything would be fine before ending the call and disconnecting. Her friend would continue to care for the animals and Maria had promised to either send someone or return herself as soon as possible.

She put away her phone and leaned against the deck rail with one hip, looking at Jesse.

"You heard all that, right?" she asked, becoming more sure of herself as the seconds passed.

Jesse nodded and stalked silently closer. "Now that the storm is over, I can have some of my guys there in a couple of hours. Unless you want to go yourself?"

She liked that he was giving her the option. "I guess I'll have to at some point, but if your men can at least secure the house for now, we can go later and see what happened there."

"Do you have to call your family? Chances are they're going to be getting visits from the *Venifucus* agents if they know about you. If they're magical at all, they could be in trouble."

"Mom has no magic. My stepdad doesn't either, but he's rich and has private security, so they're pretty well protected. My aunt and grandmother are probably still at the cabin, if they're not already on their way to Wyoming, but I don't keep their information in my house anywhere anymore. It's all in here." She tapped her temple. "Since I made friends with a werecougar and saw what she went through, she impressed on me the need for secrecy when it came to certain things. I'm glad now that I took her advice and destroyed any written record of addresses or phone numbers. Although I do keep some numbers in my smartphone. The werecougar probably wouldn't approve."

Jesse shook his head with an expression of relief. "That is good news. Just to be safe, though, I can dispatch some men to keep an eye on your mom and stepdad. And to escort your aunt and grandmother here, if you like. I know Sally would like to meet them and their magic may be needed to help heal Leonora.

You can keep your phone on. The bad guys know by now that you're with us, and they know where we live. There's nothing to be gained from trying to track your number, if they even have it."

Jesse moved closer, wrapping his big hands around her waist and leaning back to look at her while he spoke. She felt the love in every move he made toward her and knew she'd been right. Her home was here now—wherever Jesse was.

"I can try to call Mom and Nona." she offered.

"Good idea." He leaned down and kissed her gently.

She didn't know how long the kiss went on before the opening of the door from inside broke them apart. She looked around Jesse's broad shoulders to see Sally walking toward them.

"Hope I'm not interrupting," she said with a wink and a grin. "There's an impatient grizzly in there who wants to know if you're a long-lost cousin to both of us."

Maria let go of Jesse as he removed his hands from her waist and stepped back. She noted that he retrieved his phone from his pants pocket and began making calls as Sally took his place next to Maria.

What followed was a twenty-minute lesson on how to bring forth the most amazing magical glowing tree that sprouted from the ground up, like a real tree, but consisted solely of energy. It could be summoned and dismissed at will now that Maria was aware of it, and the first examination of its many branches showed that yes, indeed, Maria was related both to Sally, through Leonora, and to the weregrizzlies named Garibaldi through her father's line.

Maria was lost in the study of her personal family tree when she realized a small crowd had gathered around her and Sally. Jason had his arm around his wife's waist and Rocky was standing to one side with Jesse, seeming impressed by what he was seeing if his expression was anything to go by.

When Maria noticed him, she looked up and smiled. "Looks like I'm your long-lost cousin too, Rocco."

"My wife will be relieved to hear it. She's been feeling a little outnumbered by all the shifters up north where we live. Once things settle down, you'll have to come up for a visit."

"So your wife isn't *were*?" Maria was intrigued.

Rocky shook his head but smiled. "No, she's human. But our two boys started shifting almost from the get go. It was hard for her to get used to at first. Especially with two of them running around. Twins aren't easy to deal with. We had to fence in the backyard right away or we'd have lost them in the woods a few hundred times. That won't last long though. As soon as they learn how to climb, we're going to be in big trouble." He laughed and the other men joined in.

"I can't even imagine." Maria let the magical family tree dissipate.

"It's a shame your line doesn't seem able to shift. There are so few of us grizzlies," Rocky said thoughtfully a moment later.

"Sorry. I never really even believed in my own magic until a couple of days ago." Maria gave him a rueful smile.

"Not your fault, just an observation. You don't suppose your auntie can shift and just never mentioned it, do you?" Rocky looked hopeful.

"I'm not sure." Maria thought back to all the times her aunt had wanted to tell her more about magic and Maria had tuned her out. "Frankly, I'm going to have to apologize to her and to Nona. I've been a little rude to them about magic all these years."

Jesse smiled and put his arm around her shoulders. "They'll forgive you. I think, judging by what you've told me about them, they're going to enjoy being part of our extended Pack, don't you?"

"Yeah, I think they'll really like being able to be open about their abilities in a place where people really do believe in magic." Maria didn't even have to think about that answer. For a long time, her female relatives had been reclusive from human society, preferring to keep to themselves or spend long summers up at the cabin where they could be who they were without having to hide their differences.

The group talked about families and adjusting to Pack life for a while before Jesse's phone rang, drawing him away from the group. He returned a moment later with a grin.

"You were right about your aunt and granny not waiting for an invitation. They just showed up in town, asking where to find me."

"Oh, no. Who did they ask?" Maria dreaded the idea that her relatives were being indiscreet.

"It's okay. They apparently followed the magic to a restaurant owned and frequented by *weres*. The owner just called me. I'm sending someone down to bring them up the mountain." Jesse seemed very casual about the whole thing, but she guessed it wasn't everyday strangers were invited into the heart of Pack territory.

"I'm so sorry." She was mortified on one level and excited to see her relatives on another.

"Don't be," Jason reinforced his brother's casual attitude. "Sally wants to meet them and they'd have been invited anyway. Besides, it's kind of cool to have an eccentric auntie in the family." Jason laughed and Sally swatted his arm.

"It's really okay, Maria. Don't pay any attention to him." Sally shot her husband a mocking, dirty look. "*Were* Packs have their share of eccentrics. It's all that magic and howling at the moon."

"I hope you'll understand, but for security reasons I'm arranging this first meeting at our house, Jay," Jesse declared in a firm voice. "I don't want to expose the Pack yet, just in case her relatives take exception to our mating."

"They wouldn't," Maria objected, but in her heart she

wasn't one hundred percent certain. The safety of the Pack had to come first. Maria understood that. "Still," she went on, "it's probably for the best that I talk to them first before you guys meet them. A lot has changed in a couple of days."

The group dispersed with good wishes for Maria's family reunion. Jesse escorted Maria out to a Jeep and seated her with a kiss before moving around to the driver's side. He drove them quickly and expertly over back-country roads through some of the most beautiful woodland Maria had ever seen. Where she lived in Iowa, things were kind of flat, but out here there were ridges, foothills and mountains. Lots of interesting terrain and lovely, giant trees in an ancient forest. The magic of the place seeped into her newly awakened senses and she felt welcomed once again, by the saplings and trees. It was really an amazing feeling of coming home to a place she'd never been before.

When he pulled the Jeep around a curve near the top of a mountain they'd been climbing steadily, Maria was stunned by the natural beauty of the house set back in the woods as if it belonged there. It was made of wood, of course, with a sloping roof whose curve echoed the sighing limbs above her head. It fit. It was part of the forest in which it lived.

"This is my place. Our place now, if you want to live here." Jesse looked nervous when she tore her gaze from the house to look at his face.

She leaned across the center console to cup his stubbly face in one palm. "It's gorgeous, Jesse. And I'm content anywhere, as long as we're together."

Relief seemed to flood his expression. He leaned over to kiss her long and deep before getting out of the Jeep and jogging around to help her down from the high vehicle. He held her hand as they walked slowly toward the structure.

"I designed this place and a couple of the guys helped me build it a few years back. It has all kinds of security features that you can't really see, but you'll be safe here, Maria. Nobody will get past my guys and me."

"I believe that," she said softly, knowing he was doing his best to make her feel secure. She really appreciated that after what she'd been through the past few days.

"My men live all around slightly below this point. It just worked out that way. I was the only one willing to brave the winds up here on the peak, but I compromised and built just below the crest. The actual top of the mountain is still a few yards above us, behind the house. This way, we only get the wind from the front and sides, but the trees have really filled in to help out as a windbreak." He seemed to think about that for a moment. "Maybe they knew you were coming? Or maybe Leonora did me a favor I wasn't aware of until this moment. The woods weren't this dense when I started building up here."

Maria extended her senses and felt a little glow of residual magic. "Someone's done something here. The trees were encouraged and still carry a little bit of the magic they used. It was done with love. That, I can tell. There's a great feeling of love and protection in every tree and sapling."

"Amazing. I think maybe Leonora knew more about the future than she was letting on. Is there any foresight in your family?"

"My aunt sees things sometimes," Maria answered at once. That's probably how she knew where to come. I never told her specifically where we were going."

"It could be the grizzly influence. A lot of them are shamans. But I'm going to bet on the dryad side this time." He grinned as they mounted the steps to the front door.

He opened the door and then surprised her by scooping her up into his arms. He carried her across the threshold, then paused to kiss her breathless just inside the house. When he finally let her up for air, her head was spinning. He always seemed to have that sort of effect on her.

"Welcome home, Maria. My mate. My love." His voice was deep and heartfelt, zinging through her with emotion so strong, it brought a tear to her eye.

"Isn't he handsome?" a familiar voice sounded from outside at the bottom of the steps.

Jesse set Maria on her feet and sprung into a ready state while she took in the fact that her aunt was already here, standing beside her grandmother, backed by a very amused-looking man in fatigue pants and a black T-shirt. She thought she remembered him from her kitchen and thought his name was Arlo. He tipped his imaginary cap in her direction as he smiled.

"I brought your visitors, Alpha," Arlo said unnecessarily. I honked the horn, but I think you and your lady were otherwise engaged. He seemed to chuckle, but wisely didn't allow his mirth to be heard aloud.

Jesse shook his head and stepped back while Maria rushed down the stairs to welcome her family. They enveloped her in herb-scented hugs that were so familiar and so cherished that the tear that had threatened really did fall this time. All three women were smiling and crying after a round of fierce hugs.

When Maria looked around after the crying and hugging had come to a natural end, Jesse and the man were both gone. The front door remained open, so Maria mounted the steps, helping Nona to a seat on the wide front porch. There were wicker chairs and a small, glass-topped mosaic table that looked inviting. Maria answered her family's questions for a good twenty minutes before Jesse reappeared with a giant tea tray filled with sandwiches and beverages.

Introductions were made as Jesse joined them. He took her aunt's teasing well, but her nona seemed harder to impress. Finally, she spoke, surprising Maria with her words.

"I'm a human mage, young man. I have no shifter blood. No dryad blood," Nona said with great dignity. Maria had explained about the family tree in as much detail as she could to her very interested audience. "I was drawn to my husband by his magic, and it's good to know it was a pure magic, though he never really acknowledged it. He worked hard all his life and was killed in a freak accident that I have long considered suspicious." Maria hadn't known that, but questions had to wait until Nona was finished with whatever it was she wanted to say. "I taught my children and grandchildren what I knew, but I always sensed it wasn't quite enough for them. Their magic is quite different from mine, though we serve the same Mistress. I want you to know that I serve Mother Earth and will not tolerate anything different for my granddaughter. I want to know where you stand on the matter, young wolf, and what your intentions are."

Jesse nodded gravely, treating her eccentric granny with all the respect of an elder statesman. His gesture touched Maria more than she could say.

"Ma'am. I stand on the side of the Light. I serve the Lady in all Her forms, as do all here in my territory, in my Pack. Unlike most, I am sworn to fight Her enemies wherever I find them. I will not lie. It is dangerous work, but it is my calling and I have trained all my life to be the best I can at it. I do not go unprepared into this fight and I can protect my mate, myself, my men and my Pack. It is my sacred duty, bound by the goddess Herself."

Wow. Maria noticed the way he put her first. So did her grandmother, judging by the smile just starting to lift the corners of her mouth.

"We have an accord then. I give her into your care with a happy heart, though I could wish you were an accountant rather than a soldier. Still, Mother Earth knows what She is doing. Our Maria was always more adventurous than the rest of her generation. She will make you a good partner on your journey through life."

Maria felt the magic of her nona's benediction, and judging by the sparkle in his eyes when he met her gaze, Jesse felt it too. This was it then. They had the blessings of both families, the woods, the Pack Alphas and a whole lot of other shifters she'd met over the course of the past few days. Life wouldn't always be perfect—there was the *Venifucus* to consider, of course—but her new life with Jesse was well underway, and she couldn't wait to see where their journey together might lead.

Epilogue

That night, after introducing her relatives to Jason, Sally and Rocky, and spending a very interesting meal discussing family histories and blood lines, Jesse and Maria spent their first night together in their new home. It was everything Maria had ever hoped for and more. There was something special about being in the place they would spend a good portion of their lives. A house they would make a home. Together.

The next day, Sally came to get Maria early. She already had Nona and her aunt in the vehicle and the four women went together to a place called Yellowtail Ridge on foot. Sally interpreted what the trees told her in their song that only she could hear. Maria felt the welcome that came up to her from the very earth and the roots of the great trees and saplings all around.

Her aunt stayed silent about what she might be feeling, probably in deference to Nona, who was her mother, after all. Nona hung back when they approached a willow tree that was glowing to Maria's vision, though none of the others said they saw anything different about it.

"This is where Leonora is resting from her injuries," Sally told them. The night before she'd described the battle that had ended in the dryad being poisoned and near death in detail. Sally had used the power of the forest to encase Leonora in the trunk of this willow tree and it had promised to keep her safe until they could gather enough of the dryad's descendants to work a great undertaking of magic to free her and heal her of her grievous wounds.

Maria felt the tug on her heart when she thought about the

dryad imprisoned in the tree. If she looked very hard, she could almost see the outline of a female body held within the bosom of the willow.

"Leonora feels your presence but says you are unable to hear her," Sally reported, seeming to be listening to something only she could hear.

"You can speak to her?" Nona asked sharply.

"A little. It's hard for her with her energy so low, but from time to time she does speak to me still," Sally answered. "She's glad you're here. You too, Margarita."

Nona gasped. "How does she know my name?"

"Leonora is far older than the oldest tree in this forest," Sally replied with a gentle smile. "She was able to track some of her progeny and watch who they married. She says she was happy when Antonio joined her line to yours. Your blood is of proud lineage and your ancestors fought alongside those who opposed the great evil in days of old."

"So my grandfather always claimed," Nona answered with a tear in her eye. "Much of my family history was lost when he passed. I've done the best I could with what little he was able to teach me before he left for the next realm."

"And Leonora says you've done very well. You've made Guiseppe proud."

Nona's tear fell then, running down her face in a happy little river at the message from beyond.

"We must gather all the women of our line that we can reach." Sally grew serious once more. "It will take a great deal of magic of all different flavors to free Leonora safely. And she says it's time to reunite the daughters of the dryad. Our forest magic will be needed in the times to come, as will yours, Margarita. All magic that is used for good will be welcomed into the circle."

Nona smiled like a young girl and Maria was touched by Leonora's words spoken through Sally's lips.

"Thank her for me, Sally, please. It would be my honor to

help in whatever small way I can."

"Good." Sally beamed. "You can start by calling all your grandchildren and inviting them to a family reunion."

"Done." Nona laughed and the rest of the women followed suit.

"One thing's for sure," Maria said with a giggle. "This is going to be one hell of a party."

"Magical boot camp is more like it," Sally added, sobering a bit. "If Leonora has her way. She wants us to train up our magic so the forest won't suffer while she's indisposed. And so we'll be ready when and if the time comes to fight the *Venifucus*."

"I've already seen some of what they can do. I think it's a really good idea to prepare. I got lucky this time," Maria replied. "Next time I want to be prepared as well as lucky."

Later that night, after making love to her mate, Maria told Jesse all about the hen party in the woods. He agreed with her desire to train her magic and added another facet to her plans.

"I haven't been able to give you the full tour yet, but there's a fully operational dojo a short walk from here where all my men train. I think the women should make use of it as well. You know as well as I do that when and if the *Venifucus* come, they won't care if you're male, female or even a child. We can add some aikido classes for fun and hopefully train up a lot of the wives and kids while we prepare them for the worst-case scenario."

"I'd love to be part of that," Maria enthused. "But at some point we have to go back to Iowa so I can clean up, pack the rest of my stuff and turn over the sanctuary to someone else."

"You could also set up a vet practice here. Even a sanctuary of sorts, if you really want it. We often try to help some of the wild ones who live in our territory if they get into trouble. You could be a big help with that."

She sat up and leaned on his bare chest, feeling excited for the possibilities of her new life. She'd thought she wouldn't be able to continue her veterinary practice, but she should have realized that Jesse would find a way for her to fulfill all her potentials.

"Can I? Really?" She stroked his chest, eager to hear his answer. "It wouldn't be as big as what I had in Iowa, but a small practice would be really wonderful."

"While I'm at it, is there anything else I can do to repair the damage I did to your peaceful life?" He laughed. "I've got the dojo so you can continue with your aikido. I'll build you an animal hospital with my own hands if I have to. I've given you my house, my forest, my Pack, and most of all...my heart."

"If I have your heart—" she leaned in to kiss him, "—I really don't need anything else at all."

About the Author

Bianca D'Arc has run a laboratory, climbed the corporate ladder in the shark-infested streets of Manhattan, studied and taught martial arts, and earned the right to put a whole bunch of letters after her name, but she's always enjoyed writing more than any of her other pursuits. She grew up and still lives on Long Island, where she keeps busy with an extensive garden, several aquariums full of very demanding fish, and writing her favorite genres of paranormal, fantasy and sci-fi romance.

Bianca can be reached through Facebook, her Yahoo group (http://groups.yahoo.com/group/BiancaDArc) or through the various links on her website (http://biancadarc.com).

He can give her anything and everything she needs—except a future.

Quinn's Quest
© 2012 N.J. Walters
Legacy, Book 4

Kidnapped and held in a crazy doctor's underground laboratory, Bethany Morris only manages to escape because Chrissten, one of her fellow abductees, creates an opportunity—by shifting into a werewolf.

Bethany's desperate for help, but who'll believe her story? The police? That'll just buy her a one-way ticket to a padded room—because here's the kicker: she's discovered she's a half-breed werewolf. Her only hope is to find Chrissten's brother.

Quinn Lawton's long, grinding search for his missing twin has turned up nothing...until Bethany rekindles his hope. Something else catches flame too—her heat cycle and a searing attraction branded with the word *mate*. Yet with so much blood on his hands, any future he might offer is already tainted beyond redemption.

Desperate for Quinn's touch alone, Bethany has no choice but to take Quinn up on his offer to quell her terrifying need, no strings attached. And hope that as the search for Chrissten intensifies, the battle with their personal demons doesn't destroy their razor-thin chance at forever.

Warning: This book contains heartbreak and love found, a crazy scientist and his werewolf flunky and a tortured werewolf hero. Plus lots and lots of steamy hot sex!

Available now in ebook and print from Samhain Publishing.

It's all about the story...

Romance

HORROR

www.samhainpublishing.com

CPSIA information can be obtained
at www.ICGtesting.com
Printed in the USA
FFOW05n0739250614

9 781619 222809